Neo Chongqing Glitch

A Cyberpunk Crime Thriller Novella

W.J. Sam

Heliopolis Press

PREQUEL NOVELLA

METAVERSE DETECTIVES

NEO CHONGQING GLITCH

W.J. SAM

About The Series

Metaverse Detectives

In the Neo Era of 2048, humanity thrives in metaverses—virtual environments that have given rise to unprecedented forms of crimes.

She Lo Ke, a wired, nerdy game geek turned detective, and his partner, Dr. Qu, navigates the sprawling, cyberpunk metropolises in the world, solving futuristic crimes in ways that defy imagination.

The Metaverse Detectives series is a metaphysical science fiction blend of detective crime, suspense, and mystery, by the author, W. J. Sam. It combines witty banter with classic tropes and intricate cyberpunk world-building. Perfect for fans of Sherlock Holmes and Cyberpunk 2077.

This is a work of fiction.

Names, characters, places, and incidents either are products of the author's imagination or are used fictitiously. Any similarity to actual events or locales or persons, living or dead, is entirely coincidental.

Neo Chongqing Glitch

Copyright © 2024 by W.J Sam

All rights reserved.

No part of this publication may be reproduced, distributed, or transmitted in any form or by any means, including photocopying, recording, or other electronic or mechanical methods, without the prior written permission of the publisher, except in the case of brief quotations embodied in critical reviews and certain other noncommercial uses permitted by copyright law.

Published by

HELIOPOLIS PRESS

Unit B, 12F, 28 Yee Wo Street, Causeway Bay, Hong Kong

www.heliopolis.press

Heliopolis Press® is a registered trademark of

Heliopolis Creative and Culture Limited

www.heliopolis-cc.com

The Hong Kong Public Library has cataloged the **paperback** edition as follows:

Name: Sam, W.J.. Author.

Title: Neo Chongqing Glitch / W.J. Sam.

Description: First edition. | Hong Kong: Heliopolis Press, 2024.

Identifiers: ISBN 978-988-70531-4-9 (eBook)

Identifiers: ISBN 978-988-70531-6-3 (Hardcover)

Subjects: Science Fiction | Mystery

Classification: F | Fiction

ISBN 978-988-70531-3-2 (Paperback)

First Edition: November, 2024

First Hardcover Edition: November, 2024

Printed in Hong Kong

Our books may be purchased in bulk for promotional, educational, or business use. Please contact your local bookseller or the Heliopolis Press Sales Department by email at sale@heliopolis.press

Contents

Dedication	VIII
Preface	IX
Epigraph	1
1. A Flying Taxi	2
2. And Then There Were None	7
3. Layered Illusions	19
4. Amateur Detective	55
5. Author's Confession	83
Epilogue	91
Afterword	94
About the author	96
Acknowledgements	97
Copyrights	98

A tribute to all the scientists and engineers who have made tangible contributions to the technological advancements depicted in this book.

Preface

Neo Chongqing Glitch is a prequel novella to the "Metaverse Detectives" series, telling the story of how the main detective protagonist meets the important police officer, Lei Yijun, during a significant event in the detective's casework. The novella was written after the first book in the series, Neo Shanghai Overdrive, and serves as a prequel with a slightly different genre focus. While the main series is presented as a sci-fi detective episodic series from the perspective of the detective, this prequel novella shifts the viewpoint of the police force, making it a subgenre of sci-fi crime and police procedure.

The main plot of Neo Chongqing Glitch (set in 2042) takes place six years before the main series (set in 2048). As such, the technological level has not yet reached my ultimate vision—technology is still evolving, leading to various problems and reflections. I aim to explore these changes through the actions and thoughts of the characters, as people of their time.

The future isn't far off, and most of the technologies mentioned in this novella should already be in the process of discovery by scientists, with some in the early stages of development. In ten years (from 2024), they will be flourishing, and in twenty years, I can confidently make some bold predictions! Stay tuned!

Through this novella, I aim to lay the groundwork for the near-future cyberpunk mystery series' world view—but not entirely! I also want to showcase a narrative driven by a core ensemble of characters. Of course,

I hope to spark readers' interest by using the well-known "modern cyber metropolis" of Chongqing as the entry point. If you're worried that this important city might be limited to a novella—don't fret! Every major future city won't just be a one-off stage; after being introduced, they will form part of a world-class metaverse stage!

The future I envision is not one of hard-boiled detectives fighting against mega-corporations, though they do exist. However, in a more realistic setting, these corporations may not appear as "evil" as they do in games. But hush, this isn't a secret—they are already part of our lives! So, what can we do? Let's see how the characters in the book will handle it!

That's all for the preface. I hope you approach these mysterious future cities and the strange cases within them with a mindset of discovering the future world!

By the way, as the author is from Hong Kong, British English spelling is used throughout this series (unless an American character appears with dialogue). Most characters are of Asian descent, so unless otherwise specified, their surnames will appear before their given names. If you encounter a character with an Asian name where the given name comes first, they are likely an overseas-born Asian. Western-background characters will use the typical Western name order. Though, many non-native Chinese speakers in Hong Kong adopt a Chinese name for convenience, so it's also possible to encounter cases where those who have lived in Hong Kong for a long time might reverse the order of their names. While this prequel doesn't explore cultural differences and name order tricks, I've made this statement to avoid potential misunderstandings.

Lucem tenebris illustrat, rationem aperit;
Causas aequat, iustitiam restituit.
Oculis acutis, veritas nescit falli;
Virtus in orbe regnat, sapientia sine fine.

Chapter 1
A Flying Taxi

In the drizzling mist of the night, the lights of *Hongyaddong* blazed brilliantly.

A man rushed through the scene, paying no attention to the marvel of human ingenuity glowing around him. He shoved his way through a dense crowd of tourists, all jostling for photos, indifferent to the biting wind and pouring rain.

"It's 2036, and they still can't get enough of this!" he grumbled as he broke free of the throng and headed up the stairs.

Reluctantly, he resigned himself to sharing a ride—waiting for a personal ride-hailing car might leave him stranded until midnight.

The rain intensified. Leaning against the railing of the platform where passengers boarded, he swiped hopelessly at the rain-soaked screen of his sleek mobile terminal. The licence plate on the display blurred beneath the water.

"What a cursed night!" he swore under his breath.

Just then, a yellow-and-black taxi drifted to a hover in front of him, like some mechanical saviour descending from the heavens. Inside, the shadowy forms of two passengers—one male, one female—sat in the back seat, their faces barely visible.

Without a second thought, the man reached out and tapped his terminal to unlock the passenger door. He was about to climb in—until he saw something that sent ice through his veins.

Two figures occupied the back seat, but they sat unnervingly still, their faces vacant, their clothes streaked with strange mud.

A wave of rot and rust hit his nostrils.

As he stood frozen, the young man closest to him turned his head with a stiff, mechanical motion. "Are you getting in?" he asked, his voice grinding, unnatural.

The young woman next to him, who seemed asleep, slumped as the taxi shifted. Her head rolled off her shoulders and disappeared into the crevice between the seats.

Horrified, the man slammed the door shut and stumbled backward, tumbling off the platform, suspended as it was on the 17th floor. He didn't even scream—only gasped as the torrential rain poured into his open mouth.

The taxi rocked, then, as if nothing had happened, floated away into the night.

Moments later, a white ride-hailing car arrived, far too late to be of comfort. Inside, a group of young party-goers, reeking of alcohol, pressed against the windows. They waved eagerly at the man, who collapsed onto the wet ground.

"Hey, mate! You alright? Need some help?"

The man, still in shock, tried to gather himself, but his words came out as a jumbled mess.

"What's wrong with him?"

"Call the police?"

The group hesitated, their hands hovering over the emergency button on the self-driving car. Then they heard the man shout, panic rising in his voice, "Yes! Call the police! Now! There's a murderer!"

Startled, the group slammed the door shut and frantically hit the alarm button, shouting into the interface, "Some lunatic's saying he is a murder!"

Sirens blared in the distance, and a patrol flyer swooped into view moments later.

"Where's the crazy one?" the officer on the flyer asked.

"There! Over there!" The ride-hailing car moved to hover above a nearby building across the canyon.

"Officer, I've been filming him the whole time. He won't escape!" one of the girls said, half trembling, half thrilled, her phone still trained on the drenched man below.

The officer signalled them to stay put while he called for backup. He then flew over to the platform, shining his light on the scene.

A lone, middle-aged man sat drenched on the platform, unmoving.

When the man saw the officer approaching, he didn't seem afraid. Instead, with a strange calmness returning to his face, he rose and said in a clear voice, "Officer, there's been a murder."

The officer frowned, confused. There was no sign of aggression or escape. The man didn't appear dangerous, but something about the scene felt off. Stepping off his flyer, the officer lifted his helmet's visor and approached, prepared to ask more questions.

That was when the man "lost it."

He let out a wild scream and collapsed into violent convulsions, thrashing on the ground.

The arriving backup officers called for an ambulance. The medics carried the man away, leaving the police to investigate the area.

But they found nothing unusual. When they questioned the group who reported the incident, all they got was a confused statement about a man yelling "murder."

The police were ready to dismiss the case as a false alarm until a sudden emergency alert came through:

At 7:23 p.m., an unmanned taxi crashed on Nanshan. All patrols were to heighten their alert levels in case of a suspected terrorist attack.

But no attack came that night.
Only a single unmanned taxi, after grazing the bustling streets of *Yuzhong* and skimming the towers of *Dongshuimen Bridge*, plummeted into the shadowy valley of *Nanshan Park*.
The following day, the authorities released a statement attributing the crash to a malfunction in the taxi company's control systems, closing the case as a public safety incident.
The man who reported the murder saw the news from his hospital bed. Hysteria overwhelmed him, and he passed out again.
The city returned to its normal bustling state as if nothing had occurred.
After a few sessions of counselling, the man no longer dreamed of that night. But he never again set foot in any form of vehicle, which made life in the hilly city unbearable.
This man left Chongqing, his home city, hoping to escape the nightmares that still haunted his mind.
He thought he had.
Six years later, an interactive 5D film, hailed as a milestone in immersive entertainment, premiered on a flourishing Metaverse server. The setting: Chongqing.
Yearning for a taste of home, the man decided to watch it. He didn't expect the film's description to awaken old terrors buried deep inside him...

The Doomed Love of Mountain City

> The tragic story of two android lovers, oppressed by their employers, searching for freedom and love... Based on the infamous 2036 Chongqing Flying Taxi Incident. Audiences can freely explore the projection layers, following the protagonists' journey to uncover the truth of life itself.

"It was all fake... Was the fake pretending to be real? Or the real pretending to be fake?"

The man went mad.

He wasn't the only one.

The film studio profited a good fortune, and the production team became famous.

The taxi company, on the other hand, faced a furious public backlash, and a related android manufacturer found itself under intense scrutiny. The authorities reopened their investigation.

Although no humans had died in the crash, the film had given the androids a humanity that sparked a fierce debate over the rights of synthetic beings.

This once-forgotten case, now the subject of fevered public discourse, ended up in the hands of Inspector Lei Yijun.

Six years ago, Lei had been the first to respond to that fateful call, only to find nothing. Today, as he sat in a special training course for the "Special Tech-Crimes Action Team," he had expected to deal with some cross-server investigation in the Metaverse. Instead, reality had delivered a painful blow.

The case had left scars on more than just the man who had reported it.

As Lei opened the digital files on his terminal, a knot of unease settled in his chest. The same sensation he had felt six years ago had returned—this time, stronger.

Chapter 2
And Then There Were None

31 August 2042, *Interview and Behind-the-Scenes Highlights from The Doomed Love of Mountain City*

A gust of wind disturbed the tranquillity of the cloud platform as an autonomous taxi descended vertically from the sky, carrying the film's two lead actors. These vehicles were a common sight for the local audience: resembling a traditional four-wheeled car but equipped with spherical omni-directional hover modules where wheels should have been. The cabin was slightly sleeker and more rounded than conventional cars. On flat surfaces, the "hover spheres" acted as wheels, but in flight, they transformed into thrusters providing lift.

The lucky audience members and media invited to the event formed a circle, watching as the two leads, at the host's invitation, leaped gracefully from the vehicle, their movements fluid and expressions lively as they waved to the crowd.

The humans erupted in a mix of cheers and astonishment: were they really humanoids?

After some friendly banter between the host and the crew, the director and the original author became the focus of the cameras.

"We created this work not just to showcase cutting-edge technology through a visual and auditory feast but also to provoke thought about technology's role in our lives. Mr Wang Yuming's original story was a tremendous inspiration to me," the director said.

Wang Yuming, the unassuming author, was an average-looking middle-aged man whose only distinguishing feature was his glasses. He replied, "The film's visual effects and immersive atmosphere have elevated the story to another level. I was worried my exploration of humanoids and the humanisation of intelligent machines wouldn't translate well, but they nailed it! Full marks to the team!"

The host chimed in, "So, Mr Wang, your novel is partially based on real events. How accurate would you say the depiction is?"

"120%," Wang Yuming answered without hesitation. "Every detail from the real case is reflected in the work!"

The director, eager to assert himself, interjected, "Although, sir, you might have got one thing wrong. We had to fix it during filming."

"Oh? What was that?"

"You can't have Hongyadong and Dongshuimen Bridge in the same frame!"

Wang Yuming didn't seem bothered by the correction. With a meaningful smile, he quipped, "The script was written that way. Full marks."

The crowd erupted into laughter, including the two humanoid actors. People seemed increasingly comfortable treating them as one of their own.

The actors laughed heartily, and the camera zoomed in for a close-up of their faces.

The scene froze on this frame.

Lei Yijun was reminded of his meeting with his superior the previous day.

"Yijun," his boss had said, "this case is yours now. Do you know why it's being reopened?"

"Because I didn't uncover the truth back then?" Lei Yijun dared not meet the older man's gaze.

"Wrong! Back then, you were just a rookie, fresh out of the academy, responding to a routine call. After the case was classified as a major traffic incident, it was out of your hands. What did you do wrong?"

"Then... is it because of public pressure now?"

"That's part of it. But more importantly, the truth matters—to us, to humanity itself! Crime is the product of human malice disrupting society. If robots can harbour 'malice,' then it's game over!"

"Ah... so—" Lei Yijun's eyes widened as understanding dawned.

"Exactly. If it was an accident, we'll hold the responsible party accountable. If it was sabotage, we'll catch the culprit. Understand? The police's job is to tackle human crimes."

"But... but what if—what if humanoids *do* have malice?"

"How would you even prove something like that? That's a problem for the world's top scientists and philosophers to argue about. Let them. Our job is straightforward. By the way, there's a scientist from Beijing in your special team this time. She's here to collect data; just cooperate with her."

"Yes, sir. Understood."

Initially, his superior's words had bolstered Lei Yijun's resolve. But after watching the film and reviewing its related materials today, doubts crept in.

As he pondered, the alarm for his meeting rang. Donning his visual sensors, Lei Yijun logged into the virtual conference room for the case.

"There were multiple strange elements. Why wasn't this pursued further back then?" Yin Xiaolin, a young forensic tech officer, questioned Lei Yijun sharply in the virtual meeting room.

Inspector Lei avoided meeting the gaze of this younger colleague, only a few years his junior. As he glanced at the two distinct factions within the team, his headache intensified. A bead of sweat rolled down his clean-shaven cheek.

The newly formed *Special Tech-Crimes Action Team* was in chaos. With no breakthroughs in the case, the members argued incessantly, each clinging to their own theories. Suddenly, Yin's pointed question shifted the entire room's attention to the previously ignored team leader.

All eyes scrutinised the medium-built, slim, and neatly groomed young man with a no-nonsense buzz cut, smooth-shaven jaw, and a pair of circular glasses perched on his face.

Lei Yijun slowly removed his glasses and pinched the bridge of his nose, exhaling deeply.

"Colleagues, senior officers," he began, "this case is proving far more complex than we expected. I understand the pressure from above to solve it within a week is immense, and I admit my inexperience as a first-time leader. However, all witnesses and evidence have been re-examined. Perhaps we should review the case again?"

Yin Xiaolin, the first proponent of the "human interference" theory, immediately raised her hand to speak. With a wave of her hand, she projected forensic evidence images and investigation reports into the virtual space.

"The only preserved evidence is a partially damaged humanoid head and a few other fragments of robotic parts. The vehicle wreckage has long since been cleared, with only the forensic reports remaining. Six years later, many physical traces are now beyond investigation. Our leads rely solely on archived road surveillance footage, along with video data provided by the taxi and humanoid companies. The lack of substantial evidence is highly suspicious—someone clearly tampered with the scene!"

Her sharp gaze fixated on Lei Yijun, as if accusing him of failing to push for further investigation back then. There was a trace of disdain in her eyes.

Although her criticisms were valid, they weren't the source of Lei Yijun's headache. Instead, he was grateful she had raised these points.

"You're absolutely right," Lei Yijun affirmed. "The evidence preservation at the time was far from ideal. Back then, with no human injuries, the incident was treated as an unmanned traffic accident. Ownership disputes over the humanoid and vehicle were resolved quickly, and no criminal case was filed. The video footage from the humanoid robot wasn't even retrieved until this reinvestigation began."

Yin Xiaolin tilted her head, arms outstretched, her stiff smile betraying her frustration. She knew the sole preserved evidence—the humanoid head—was untampered with, sealed securely in the forensics department's archive. The lack of video retrieval back then wasn't because of technological limitations but rather the premature closure of the case.

Holographic projections replayed scans of the evidence alongside the extracted footage on a loop in the meeting room.

"I agree with the young lady—someone must have tampered with the evidence. But you're all overthinking it," interjected Xia Wenqiang, an unkempt veteran officer with a scruffy beard, arms crossed as he shook his head. "I know little about tech; I solve cases with gut and experience. To me, robots are just machines, like cars. The key here is who first 'maliciously manipulated' them to cause the accident."

Yin Xiaolin, still tilting her head, spun in place to face a man leaning silently against the wall.

The man was in his early forties, streaks of unnatural white in his hair betraying years of overthinking. This was Ge Renjie, a senior officer with higher rank and longer service than anyone else in the room. However, stationed outside Chongqing and preoccupied with other major cases, he hadn't taken the team lead position.

Yin Xiaolin, dissatisfied with Lei Yijun's lack of experience, was clearly hoping Ge would speak up.

The case was uniquely challenging: apart from the taxi company being local, the car's control systems, the humanoid development and operations companies, the film studio, and even the key witnesses were all based elsewhere. One crucial witness outright refused to cooperate in person. Were it not for the case's high profile, these evidentiary hurdles would have been insurmountable.

"There's no need to let the pressure weigh us down," Ge Renjie finally spoke. "This is a test run for the 'Special Tech-Crimes Action Team' mechanism. As you all know, in the age of the metaverse, the Internet of Things has permeated every aspect of our physical lives, while the traditional internet has evolved into a more advanced virtual space. Many crimes now transcend regional and even national boundaries. If we don't modernise our investigative methods, we'll fall behind criminals rooted in virtual and cross-border domains."

Ge's position aligned with Yin Xiaolin's and Xia Wenqiang's—they all believed the incident resulted from deliberate human interference. However, the specific methods remained unclear, leaving them to rely on their individual expertise to investigate.

On the opposing side were Lei Yijun and two less familiar team members.

"Could it simply have been a software or mechanical malfunction?" Shi Qingxuan, a criminal psychologist and proponent of the "mechanical failure," theory, calmly countered. "It's a more natural and straightforward explanation. We can't let the investigation be influenced by the film's narrative. If there was human interference, the focus should be on how the companies involved handled the aftermath. Who's hiding the truth? And who's exploiting the situation?"

The "mechanical failure" camp wasn't entirely unified, splitting into "accident cover-up" and "pure coincidence" factions.

Representing the latter, forensic specialist Xue Zhiming straddled a chair backward, resting his chin in his hands, eyes half-closed as if lost in thought. Xue had barely contributed to the investigation, his disinterest plainly written on his weary face.

Yawning, he muttered, "Spontaneous human combustion is real. Machines are even more prone to these so-called 'non-fault' mishaps. The vehicle in question used semi-solid batteries, a soon-to-be-obsolete technology with a much higher self-combustion rate than today's advanced compressed solid-state batteries. The rest is just amateurs passing blame, sensationalist media stirring the pot, and that film pandering to the masses. Robots as actors? People crying their eyes out over it? Please."

Yin Xiaolin twisted her head toward Xue, glaring at him with her piercing gaze. "The collision alarm triggered before the high-temperature alert."

Lei Yijun cleared his throat awkwardly. He was among the silent audience members moved to tears by the film's narrative.

Six years ago, Lei Yijun had sensed something off about the case but couldn't pinpoint it. When it was swiftly dismissed due to the lack of injuries, he'd felt relieved his city had returned to peace so quickly—never expecting the issue to boomerang back and hit him as the officer who had "happened" to take the initial report. Back then, before debates over humanoid mistreatment erupted, he'd thought the film was well done. Now...

Lei stared at the holographic projection of the humanoid's mangled head. Its burnt and disfigured face bore a default smile, but in that moment, it seemed to mock human incompetence.

Seeing Lei Yijun's conflicted and hesitant expression, Ge Renjie decided to help him reflect further. "How exactly do we define the 'incident'? If it was human interference, do we consider the moment the robot was damaged or the time of the taxi's crash? If it was an accident, was the malfunction sustained or momentary? Dr Wu, what's your perspective?"

Faced with the sudden question, Wu Mengyi, engrossed in analysing data on her tablet, showed no emotional reaction. In a calm voice, she explained, "I'm only here to provide technical support for the 'Di Renjie System.' If you ask for a definition, I'd call it an open-ended question—how you define it depends on the stakeholder's perspective."

To Lei Yijun, her answer was as useful as saying nothing. His frustration deepened.

"Hah! I told you this flashy tech isn't worth much!" Xia Wenqiang scoffed. "Big data restoration? Scene reconstruction? All nonsense! It's as confusing as that movie. I just know one thing: where there's smoke, there's fire, and the fire is always started by people. Let's just focus on identifying the suspects."

Dr Wu didn't react to his gruff dismissal. Instead, she silently activated the system, projecting a detailed reconstruction of the incident site.

The dim space lit up as ripples of light radiated outward, forming a lifelike 3D simulation. Two fifty-storey towers clung to opposing mountainsides, separated by a narrow mountain road. Streams of flying cars, taxis, and drones passed between them in an intricate dance. Pedestrians emerged from one tower and stepped onto mobile stairways that carried them to the other. The scene felt so real it could have been happening right in front of them.

The recreated sequence mirrored the movie: a yellow-and-black autonomous taxi carrying a trembling young couple soared through Chongqing's rain-soaked night. A heavy downpour enveloped the city in thick fog, the neon lights refracting through the haze to create an otherworldly backdrop. The car, initially following a normal outbound route, suddenly veered off course, as if overwhelmed by the intensifying rain. It swayed erratically before disappearing into the misty night over the Jialing River. The simulation sped forward thirty minutes, showing a small, faint fire flicker briefly on the distant Nanshan hillside.

"This simulation was generated from public data. Now, we'll incorporate information and visuals known only to the police," Dr Wu explained.

The 3D display updated to include flight paths for vehicles. Lei Yijun recognised the colour-coded lanes—designated for private cars, commercial vehicles, and freight drones—structured like air traffic corridors, programmed into the vehicles' control systems.

"The target vehicle followed the planned route for autonomous cars. Its journey began at 6:30 PM in the city centre and ended at approximately 7:05 PM when it abruptly changed direction. At 7:23 PM, it burned."

In the movie, this sequence had been dramatised as two humanoid robots battling the taxi's autopilot system in a desperate attempt to escape human control, culminating in the vehicle crashing into the mountainside.

"In reality, the primary incident site was not where the taxi ultimately crashed," Shi Qingxuan noted. "The first reports came from the city centre, where witnesses claimed they saw the female humanoid's head fall off. Thinking it was a human victim, the witness was traumatised."

Police reconstructions from the taxi's control system revealed that the vehicle had flown steadily for most of its journey, only plummeting near its destination.

"If there had been a struggle like in the film, there would have been irregular movements and turbulence in the vehicle's flight path," Shi continued. "Instead, the sudden change in trajectory didn't trigger any system alerts. The taxi's only warning was at 7:23 PM, right before the crash, when it sent a single 'fall alarm,' followed by an overheat signal."

Dr Wu manipulated the panel to display footage of the burned wreckage.

The simulation depicted a rainy hillside covered in mud. The fire from the crash burned briefly before being doused by the rain. A small patch of forest, rarely visited by humans, was scorched, leaving scattered robotic debris.

"Our forensic analysis matches the eyewitness accounts," Yin Xiaolin explained. "There were remains of two humanoids and the taxi, all severely burned. Fortunately, one headpiece was dislodged in the crash and landed away from the flames, preserving its memory storage."

"What about the taxi's black box? Is it completely unrecoverable?" Xia Wenqiang asked sharply.

"The taxi's communication and fault signals ceased after the overheat alert," Wu Mengyi replied.

"No onboard video or surveillance footage?" Xia pressed.

Ge Renjie projected the investigation results onto the display. Two corporate logos appeared: the orange insignia of *Momo Controls* and the blue emblem of *Humanoid House*.

"Momo Controls' safety systems were from an outdated generation and marketed with a 'privacy-first' approach. Onboard recordings were only uploaded in the event of an accident or with user consent. Unfortunately, their system lacked the robustness of an aircraft's black box. After the incident, the company faced regulatory scrutiny, causing a stock plunge and eventual bankruptcy. The founder left under a mountain of debt."

Momo's orange logo faded, replaced by the blue symbol of Humanoid House, which morphed into the image of a flying saucer.

"The humanoid manufacturer, Humanoid House, is a subsidiary of Oort Intelligence, a global tech leader," Ge continued. "Six years ago, they only filed a civil suit against Momo for property damage, which was settled out of court for a small sum. However, after Momo's collapse, Oort announced its own proprietary flight control system, which is now widely adopted by rental and private vehicles."

Xia Wenqiang clapped his hands, his face lighting up with an expression of sudden understanding. "I knew it! This reeks of—what's it called? Malicious business competition!"

Ge nodded, then shook his head. "It's a theory, but there's no evidence—none that would hold up legally—to prove that Oort manipulated humanoids to sabotage vehicles. Xiaolin, we've reviewed your team's cybersecurity report."

Lei Yijun, observing Yin Xiaolin's frustrated expression, felt a pang of sympathy. He understood her zeal to uncover the criminals' trail, driven by youthful determination and a strong sense of justice.

"If the initial cause was accidental, then the focus shifts to the cover-up," Lei offered, attempting to comfort the team. "What exactly is being concealed? Design flaws in the robots or cars? The true events of the crash? There's too much to consider. Frankly, solving this in seven days is unrealistic."

But Yin Xiaolin was clearly unmoved. She insisted on re-examining all corporate systems with the tech team.

"We have four days left. We must have a preliminary conclusion by then. Whether to continue the investigation isn't our call. For now, split into groups and work your angles. Report any updates immediately. Meeting adjourned!" Lei Yijun reluctantly made his decision.

The team dispersed, each diving into their respective tasks.

Chapter 3
Layered Illusions

Lei Yijun's senses returned to his desk, where the holographic display was cluttered with case files he had just reorganised.

"If it was human intervention, at what stage did they interfere? If it was a machine malfunction, who's been influencing the investigation?" he murmured to himself, jotting the core questions into his investigation log.

"The breakthrough... it has to be the part that felt off to me. Why did the witness react like that when they reported the incident?"

"Someone... or no one..."

The weight of responsibility had kept Lei Yijun under immense mental strain for days, robbing him of sleep. As he muttered these keywords, he drifted off into his chair.

He didn't know how long he had been asleep when a chill jolted him awake. Realising he had lost four precious hours, he leapt up, slapping his face to shake off the drowsiness. The heavy bags under his eyes were something he dared not confront in the mirror.

"Just push through! One more time!" Lei rallied himself before seeking out Wu Mengyi to learn how to make better use of the *Di Renjie System*.

"This system is designed to reconstruct environments, simulate scenarios, and visualise data analyses," Wu explained in her even tone. "It cannot replace a human investigator's judgment. It can immerse you in a simulated environment and generate real-time 5D scenarios based on hypothetical conditions. It's similar in principle to the cinematic systems, but whereas those rely on the imagination of screenwriters and directors, we aim to reconstruct factual elements."

Lei Yijun had learned some of this during his training. The *Di Renjie System*, like the widely used *Song Ci System* in forensic science, was a landmark innovation in criminal technology, leveraging smart and digital tools to upgrade investigative capabilities. While *Song Ci* specialised in extracting and analysing biological evidence, *Di Renjie* focused on integrating real-world factors and simulating all relevant information.

This case, however, had no biological evidence—everything organic had been incinerated in the fire. That was partly why the forensic pathologist, Xue Zhiming, had shown little enthusiasm; he'd been assigned to the team for training but joked about his lack of utility.

"Can you recreate all the related scenes of the case?" Lei asked.

Due to the absence of in-car footage, the system could only draw on street surveillance and operational data provided by the taxi company.

"Of course. However, I must remind you that these visuals and sounds are not the actual events. They're reconstructions based on existing evidence and testimonies. Keep that in mind when making judgments," Wu said.

Lei nodded in understanding and awkwardly donned the specially designed full-body sensory equipment. What they had seen in the meeting room earlier had been rudimentary projections, but the full 5D system would allow him to enter the fourth layer of the metaverse: the *simulacrum layer*. In this layer, a user's five senses were fully simulated through advanced sensors, earning it the name *5D projection*.

Despite his training, Lei felt a mix of nervousness and excitement at the prospect of using the system for the first time. Taking a deep breath, he started the *Di Renjie System*. His vision went black momentarily before brightening as if ink dissolving in water, the darkness giving way to clarity. Lines of floating text appeared in elegant strokes, reminiscent of a traditional Chinese calligraphy poem:

> *Lucem tenebris illustrat, rationem aperit;*
> *(He sees through veils, the hidden truths unseal'd;)*
> *Causas aequat, iustitiam restituit.*
> *(And rights the scales where justice had been marr'd.)*
> *Oculis acutis, veritas nescit falli;*
> *(With piercing sight, no falsehood stays conceal'd;)*
> *Virtus in orbe regnat, sapientia sine fine.*
> *(Fair virtue's torch shines bright, her bounds unbarr'd.)*

Before Lei could ponder the meaning of the classical text in a modern context, the electronic "ink" spread outward, painting the scene of a rainy evening six years ago in vivid detail.

The stifling humidity of a summer downpour enveloped him, turning the mountain city into a steam bath. It was around 6 PM, the transition between day and night, with the city lights yet to flicker on.

Tourists crowded scenic spots for photo opportunities, but locals bustled to get home or ducked into shopping centres to escape the rain. Restaurants along the streets were coming alive with activity. Mountain roads twisted and turned, their traffic gridlocked. Buses and metro stations were packed with lines of commuters. Flying cars were the only viable option for those in a hurry.

The cacophony of voices and the smell of rain surrounded Lei, immersing him in the simulation. Everything felt unnervingly real.

Except for one thing: as a future observer, Lei existed as a ghost-like entity, able to float, phase through walls, and teleport to any coordinate or moment. Whenever he focused on a specific spot, the system not only reconstructed the scene but overlaid floating annotations and sources of information.

"This is like a 'memory palace,'" Lei marvelled.

Though an ordinary man, without photographic memory or superhuman insight, technology had granted him a new perspective—to see the past and ponder the future.

"Let's start by observing the moment they boarded the taxi," Lei murmured.

With a gesture, he manipulated the simulation, projecting his consciousness to the moment where the nightmare began.

1: July 16, 2036, 6:01 AM, Yishan Nursing Home

Manager Zhang sat nervously, waiting for a network call. His shift was about to end, but the staff from *Humanoid House* hadn't shown up yet.

He glanced at the young man seated motionless on a chair beside him and sighed.

"You've been functioning perfectly fine up until now. What's gone wrong recently?"

Though his words were directed at the young man, there was no reaction—no flicker of emotion, not even a blink.

Just then, the doorbell for the 10th-floor platform rang. Manager Zhang immediately stood and opened the freight door.

A worker wearing a baseball cap entered, carrying a large black bag. Behind him was another young man.

"You're finally here. We're doing a replacement, not repairs, right?" Zhang asked, sounding both annoyed and relieved.

"Apologies. The company vehicle had some issues, so I had to fly slower," the worker replied apologetically.

"This is the new one?"

Zhang scrutinised the young man who had followed the worker in. He was identical to the one sitting in the chair—same face, build, and even clothing.

"They" were companion-care humanoids.

"The customised face delayed things a bit," the worker explained. "If this were a standard model, it wouldn't have taken so long. Here, please electronically sign this, and pack the relevant parts into the bag."

Zhang opened his work terminal, signing the documents with his fingerprint while issuing a command:

"Unit 37, pack your things into this bag."

Unit 37 understood the instruction, rising from its wireless charging chair with smooth, mechanical precision. It adjusted its clothing and began packing its components into the worker's bag.

"By the way, make sure you don't transfer the personalised settings yet," the worker reminded Zhang. "Disable the locator, alarms, and other trackers, then log out of your account."

Zhang followed the instructions with a flurry of actions. "Don't we need to do a factory reset?"

"Not necessary," the worker assured him. "Once you log out, all privacy data is erased. The system will ensure complete data deletion afterward. For now, we need to analyse this unit's learning model to identify any issues before formatting it. Personalised settings will be pushed to your new unit after verification."

Zhang nodded, satisfied, and turned his attention to setting up the new Unit 37.

Meanwhile, the original Unit 37 had already been decommissioned from the Yishan Nursing Home's system. It walked silently to the back of the worker's vehicle.

The worker confirmed the handover, loaded the unit, and drove away.

It wasn't until after the worker left that Zhang remembered the elderly resident served by Unit 37 had mild cognitive impairment. He quickly instructed the new unit:

"Remember, if your grandmother starts chatting with you today, just give her a mild sedative and put her to bed early. We can't have her noticing anything."

This scene struck Lei Yijun as deeply unsettling. He stared at the two service humanoids for a long time, thinking to himself: *They're absolutely identical.*

He made a point to investigate the nursing home's internal operations thoroughly but found nothing suspicious. The elderly resident served by Unit 37 had taken her sedative and peacefully fallen asleep, completely unaware her "grandson" had been replaced.

Lei fast-forwarded to the next day. The new Unit 37 appeared to have received a system update, resuming normal service without further malfunctions. From that point forward, it never left the nursing home premises.

Lei couldn't shake the eerie normalcy of it all. Even with no outward signs of anomalies, the seamless replacement of the humanoid had left an impression he couldn't ignore. Something about the perfect replication—and the casual handling of it—gnawed at him.

2: July 16, 2036, 6:12 AM, Moulin Rouge Murder Mystery Venue

An interactive murder mystery performance had just concluded. Manager Cui instructed the cleaning robots to tidy up the venue quickly to prepare for the evening show.

Meanwhile, he busied himself collecting the scattered "body parts" from the floor.

They were fragments of an actor-model humanoid—the robot's last day on the job.

After piecing together the battered machine with some effort, Manager Cui attempted a restart. However, its movements were sluggish and far from lifelike.

"Good thing I bought the warranty. These kids are downright vicious with these things," he muttered to himself.

Cui wondered if it would be more cost-effective to buy cheaper models specifically designed to play corpses. The frequent repair costs were becoming unmanageable.

This humanoid, modelled as a woman, was the most expensive one in his venue. Ever since a previous client—trying to show off—had duplexed the robot while it was playing a secret agent NPC, it hadn't functioned properly.

In its last performance earlier that day, Manager Cui had assigned it to portray a stuttering victim to make the most of its impaired state. However, the "culprit" ignored the instruction manual during the simulated "dismemberment," causing severe joint deformation that rendered the unit irreparable.

For today's show, Cui had relegated the robot to playing the role of a dismembered corpse in two separate acts. He had even mixed up some parts and was now painstakingly sorting them out.

After a while, the collection team arrived. The process followed the usual routine, though this time, the worker asked Manager Cui to help push the remains into the back of the transport truck.

"The model you ordered is currently out of stock. We'll deliver it in a few days. Apologies for the inconvenience," the worker explained.

"No problem. I'll just switch up the script for now. Just get it here as soon as you can," Cui replied.

Lei Yijun disliked the casual way this scene treated the humanoid "body." It wasn't as unsettling as the previous nursing home episode, but it left him feeling uneasy.

This type of theatre seemed popular among bored university students and stressed-out office workers. The venue operated legally, and the manager had a clear alibi. There were no suspicious details.

Nonetheless, Lei took the opportunity to have the system tag the specific number of "parts" being removed. He also noted that humanoid B's head had a loose connection, making it prone to detachment—an observation that might prove relevant later.

3: July 16, 2036, 6:24 AM, Old Chaotianmen Wholesale Market Rooftop Platform

The transport truck finally broke down. Fortunately, the rooftop platform of a nearby commercial street offered an emergency landing spot. After a bumpy descent, the vehicle landed safely.

The worker had no choice but to unload the two "packages" and call for a heavy-lift drone to tow the truck back to the company.

By now, the light drizzle had intensified into a torrential downpour. While heavy drones could still operate in such adverse conditions, the rain created misery for everything and everyone else nearby. Splashes of muddy water, like airborne dust, coated the area.

Flagging down one of the few autonomous taxis available at this hour, the worker placed the package of parts in the front seat and directed the two humanoids to enter the back.

However, he did not board the taxi himself. Instead, he programmed a flight route for it and then hailed a separate ride-share vehicle, carrying only his backpack. This second autonomous car headed in the opposite direction of the taxi.

At approximately 7:25 AM, the worker arrived back at his company's office in the northeast CBD, where he clocked in and resumed his shift.

◆

Lei Yijun pulled up the worker's file. His name was Liu Jianbin, a temporary employee who had been blamed for the mishandling of the cargo. Although he had a perfect alibi, he was dismissed by *Humanoid House* after the incident for negligence during transport.

The records noted his reason for not accompanying the taxi: "wanted to get home early to shower and change clothes."

Despite his airtight alibi, Lei marked Liu Jianbin as "suspicious." As one of the few humans with close contact with the humanoids involved in the case, he couldn't be overlooked.

4: July 16, 2036, 6:37 AM, 17th-Floor Platform of a Serviced Apartment near Daronghui

As the weather worsened, Li Deqing was stood up by a client. Disappointed, he left a trendy hotpot restaurant near a famous tourist spot. Eating hotpot alone wasn't appealing, so after hurriedly grabbing some street food, he hailed a taxi home.

Li worked a high-paying job in finance and was accustomed to commuting in comfort. Despite the heavy rain, he avoided the metro, hoping to secure a luxury ride. However, with vehicle availability stretched thin, he wandered aimlessly, eventually seeking shelter at a serviced apartment he had previously arranged for clients. He remembered the building had a private drop-off platform, less crowded than the street, and thought he might have better luck there.

This frustrating end to a stressful day compounded his foul mood. Already under immense workplace pressure, Li had been taking mood stabilisers, which he nearly forgot to use in the chaos.

As he waited on the platform, an autonomous taxi descended before him, its rear seats already occupied. Li, hindered by the heavy rain, didn't check his terminal to confirm the ride and assumed it was his car.

But just as he approached the vehicle, he witnessed something horrifying: one of the muddy, rain-drenched figures in the back seat—a young man or woman—had their head fall off!

The sight triggered an immediate psychological episode. Li collapsed onto the platform in a daze, his condition worsening as his body trembled uncontrollably.

What happened next was a blur to him. Security footage from the apartment showed him ranting incoherently at the young responding officer, who arrived on the scene. Moments later, Li lost consciousness, and paramedics arrived to rush him to the hospital.

Lei Yijun watched this segment repeatedly from different angles, treating it as a critical piece of the puzzle.

From the reconstructed footage, the vehicle's interior was too obscured to make out clear details. It was reasonable for a highly stressed witness like Li Deqing to miss anything suspicious until he opened the door and saw something shocking.

Yet Lei couldn't make sense of one key detail: why had the witness suffered such an acute episode after Lei himself arrived at the scene? What could have provoked Li's sudden seizure-like reaction?

After the incident, Li Deqing had left Chongqing, citing the trauma as too overwhelming to remain in the city. He had been uncooperative during this reopened investigation, refusing further involvement.

Could Inspector Ge convince him to engage? Lei couldn't shake the feeling that Li Deqing might hold a crucial piece of the truth.

5: July 16, 2036, 6:52 AM, Passenger Flight Zone Near Dongshuimen Bridge

The yellow-and-black autonomous taxi followed the designated flight path for small passenger drones, flying at a height above the bridge deck but below the main towers of the bridge.

The bridge lights had yet to illuminate, and the surroundings were shrouded in a rainy haze that significantly reduced visibility. Some airborne vehicles collided mid-flight, forcing emergency landings on the bridge deck below.

None of this, however, involved the target vehicle.

As the taxi neared the midpoint of the bridge, it executed a turn.

Despite the heavy rain, the vehicle's operation appeared entirely normal from an external perspective. It maintained a steady altitude during the first part of its journey, executed a sudden but controlled turn near the bridge's centre, and began a gradual descent as it approached its destination.

In contrast, manually piloted flying vehicles in the area exhibited noticeable lateral disturbances and erratic movements because of the adverse weather.

Chaos and order seemed to coexist harmoniously within the same city.

Lei Yijun, fortunate to have no fear of heights, heeled the trajectory of the flying taxi during the simulation.

Throughout the journey, the vehicle showed no signs of collisions or unusual signals.

The forensic team's report had definitively ruled out the possibility of the humanoids hacking into the taxi's control system. Additionally, there was no evidence of the taxi being remotely operated.

Nearby small flying vehicles were unaffected by similar disturbances, and their flight paths did not intersect with the trajectory of the accident vehicle.

Lei annotated this segment as likely representing a pre-programmed route rather than an internal physical altercation. He noted no visible signs of external interference. The vehicle's trajectory appeared deliberate, planned, and undisturbed.

6: July 16, 2036, 7:13 AM, Above the Forested Slope Near Nanshan Tunnel

Due to the heavy rain, the vehicle's speed was slower than average, as it took longer to travel than it would on a clear day. After the course was adjusted, the flow of traffic around the vehicle noticeably diminished, and it headed almost directly toward its destination.

The small car entered the Nanshan region and, just as it seemed to decelerate and land, it shook violently with extreme forward and backward tilts.

After rolling and swaying for a while, the vehicle's rear end scraped the tops of the trees before crashing into an uninhabited forested area.

◈

Regarding the last crash, the police report from six years ago, upon closing the case, relied on flight detection and surveillance records around Nanshan Park. These findings aligned with the simulations: the vehicle had lost balance before the crash. A large fire broke out after the vehicle struck the ground, and the taxi company was held primarily accountable.

During the roll and tumble, several objects had been ejected from the vehicle. Because of the slope of the hillside, many of these objects—including a crucial piece of evidence—were found along the edge of the flatter road below the hill.

Lei Yijun attempted to search the forest from his own perspective, trying to land within the area. However, he failed. The area of the forest without pathways was a surveillance blind spot, meaning the system had only simulated a normal night-time forest scene.

Officer Lei recorded this blind spot issue in his log.

July 16, 2036, Residual Video from B's Head Fragment

A visual signal, devoid of sound, gradually became clearer as it was extracted from beneath the backseat of a car by a pair of hands.

The head was mounted onto a cylindrical support and secured, fixing the view. The video content stabilised as the perspective became locked in place.

The view ahead showed the dim interior of the vehicle's front seat and the blurred, rain-soaked scenery outside.

The left side of the vehicle was out of the frame, with only occasional glimpses of the nearest main pillar of a suspension bridge visible.

On the right side of the frame, the edge occasionally revealed the side profile of a man, his face caked in mud. Like the head, he remained perfectly still. Throughout the entire footage, he did not move once.

At 6:52 AM, the vehicle sharply veered to the right by about 130°. The bridge disappeared from the left side of the frame, and the view ahead turned completely black, save for rain pouring down and faint, eerie light filtering in from an odd angle.

After continuing for some time, the vehicle suddenly jolted with a sharp lurch, causing the head to fall from its mount, spinning violently. The signal cut out after the power was lost.

This was the last frame, time-stamped at 7:22 AM.

◈

The first-person perspective made Lei Yijun feel dizzy and nauseous, almost to the point of vomiting. Although he wasn't sure whether his body would react the same way in this immersive simulation state, the sensation of motion sickness was overwhelming.

He made a firm decision to never watch this footage again.

It seemed the video had been preserved because B's head had been impacted. Two collisions had caused the recording function to shut down and restart. From the footage, only one conclusion could be drawn: during the drive after the doors closed, there was no external intrusion, and there were no visible mechanical malfunctions or signs of criminal activity inside the vehicle.

NEO CHONGQING GLITCH

This is the real-time simulation of the crime scene and the specific video evidence.

Lei Yijun called up a bird's-eye view of the entire city, instructing the system to mark key locations in mid-air.

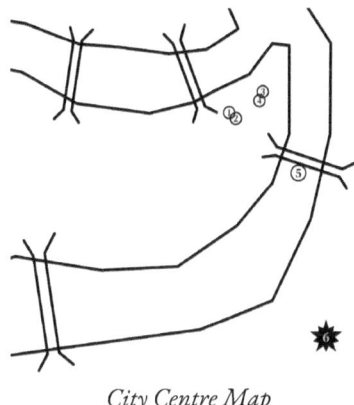

City Centre Map

He mentally mapped out the major phases of the case: the parts involving people were when the two managers of the androids returned the products needing repairs to the employees of the android company — during which employee negligence played a role. The parts involving no one were from when the incident was witnessed by the bystander. The car door closed, and then the crash.

The dividing point was the witness's observation.

There was a period during which no interior footage of the car existed, but because of the bustling environment it was flying through, even a flying vehicle would have had its exterior fully captured by surveillance cameras. Despite the loss of the vehicle's stored 360-degree footage, the external data from the surroundings were intact.

Up in the simulation layer, high above the city, Lei Yijun felt an unsettling chill, a sense of unease that didn't match the environment: the city itself felt like a massive, surveillance-formed prison!

This was all the evidence related to the mystery from six years ago. Yet, in the back of his mind, Lei Yijun recalled Dr Wu's warning: *These are only simulations based on evidence and testimonies!*

Lei Yijun was more certain than ever that someone was concealing crucial information. Next, he planned to include that controversial film in his reference materials.

"Doctor, we can exit the scene reconstruction now. Let's move to the next stage."

With that, Lei Yijun's senses returned to the real world. He could distinctly feel his body shift from the damp environment of the simulation back into the dry, cold laboratory.

However, his vision remained in the third layer of the metaverse — the projection layer. Here, Officer Lei would continue his investigation, examining the relevant third-party files tied to the case.

July 17, 2036 Police Incident Report [Text]

On the evening of July 16, between 7:00 PM and 8:00 PM, a crash involving an autonomous flying taxi occurred near the Nanshan Scenic Area in our city. Currently, there are no reported injuries or fatalities. Initial investigations have identified the incident as a mechanical failure, resulting in a traffic accident.

(Social media safety tips from traffic police attached) We urge all users of autonomous driving systems and licensed operators of flying vehicles to prioritise safety during operation and adhere to the mandated regular vehicle maintenance schedules.

July 17, 2036 - Online Media Coverage of the Incident

(Footage from a handheld recording device)

In the dim light of a night where the heavy rain had finally subsided, a burnt forest was crowded with people. Firefighters and police officers had completely cordoned off the smoking area.

The actual firefighting operations were primarily conducted by drones and fire-prevention robots, but their intelligence clearly wasn't sufficient to manage the growing crowd of onlookers.

Beyond the layers of officials was a throng of people gathered outside the forest. Some were journalists who had rushed to the scene, others were amateur content creators filming indiscriminately, and a few were passersby who stumbled across the commotion.

A firefighter with a megaphone shouted loudly: "The fire is fully extinguished! But the smoke could be toxic! Everyone, stay back!"

The individual filming was evidently stuck in the outermost layer of the crowd, unable to get closer. Upon hearing the warning, the surrounding onlookers scattered in a panic. The person filming also retreated down the hill and concluded the video with a brief commentary by the roadside.

Beneath the short video, bold, attention-grabbing text read:*"**Autonomous Taxi Crashes in Nanshan, Possibly Releasing Toxic Gas. Crowds Flee in Panic."** [Shocking!]*

Watching this, Lei Yijun couldn't help but pinch his thigh.

"Now *this*... is journalism."

February 5, 2037 - Afternoon, Video Conference with a Film Company

On one side of the video conference was the smiling face of a seasoned producer, exuding eagerness; on the other was the calm and confident demeanour of the original author, Wang Yuming.

"Mr Wang, do you find this level of adaptation acceptable? Adding a bit of intense romance could really generate buzz. If the budget is agreeable, we can move forward and sign the film contract," the producer asked impatiently.

"Of course. I believe your 5D simulation technology has the potential to captivate audiences worldwide. Only the latest innovations can push the boundaries of human imagination, transforming words into reality. I'm fully on board with a certain degree of commercial adaptation. However—"

The screen showing Wang Yuming froze for a moment.

The producer, unsure if it was a network glitch or if there was truly a dreadful "however" coming, grew visibly more anxious. She fidgeted with her interface to fix the issue, but before she could act further, Wang Yuming resumed speaking.

"My main job keeps me very busy, so I won't have much time to supervise the script. I trust you'll achieve the promised adaptation quality."

"Are you still working as a journalist?"

"Of course. It's a fascinating job and a great source of inspiration. This work itself came from ideas sparked during my assignments. Oh, by the way, you'll likely need authorisation from Oort, won't you? They're long-time clients of mine. One condition of this adaptation is to feature Oort's latest humanoid actor models as the lead characters."

The producer nodded enthusiastically, her grin widening to the point of splitting her face. "That's absolutely fine! Those new models are way out of budget for most productions."

"I'll also write a few exclusive on-set reports for you afterward, maximising the buzz around the project. Here's to a fruitful collaboration," Wang Yuming said with a polite nod.

"You really know the business! Of course, here's to a great partnership," the producer replied.

※

Oort!

The name rang a bell for Lei Yijun. He had recently heard it during Ge Renjie's briefing, and now it resurfaced with sharp familiarity. Lei was certain that after the incident, Oort had undertaken several actions to align with its commercial interests, including leveraging the film's breakout success and stirring public discussion.

As for whether Oort had manipulated anything prior to the incident, Lei believed the key lay in investigating the dismissed temp worker. He could only wait for Detective Xia's report to delve further into this thread.

Lei Yijun finally pulled up the original novel behind the controversial movie for review. He wasn't a literary analyst, nor did he know if the story's content could serve as evidence in the investigation. Still, he decided to endure his poor impression of Wang Yuming and read it for a broader understanding of the case's dimensions.

Excerpt from the Novella *The Doomed Love of Mountain City*
Author: Wang Yuming

1

Grandma often told me stories about the world outside, and gradually, I came to know many things about it from her.

There were mountains, skyscrapers, beautiful rivers, magnificent bridges, and many restaurants Grandma used to love.

"You little things are getting worse at cooking!" she would complain frequently.

The doctors didn't allow her to eat anything too stimulating, so I had to stop her and her old friends from sneaking suspicious snacks into the facility with drones.

Not that it made much difference. Grandma said that her generation didn't have as many rules, so she just went her own way—like today, when she was off to play mahjong with her friends. No doubt they'd exchange these "childhood treasures" with each other.

I'd heard that even the administrators turned a blind eye to their antics and sometimes brought them a few extra bags of snacks. All this, of course, was under the watchful eye of the intelligent security system, S.

But so what? They wouldn't get into real trouble—at most, they'd endure a scolding from the doctors.

On the afternoons, when I didn't have to look after Grandma, I'd watch films or dramas alone in my room. Grandma often liked to chat about the stories, so I had to study them in advance to avoid fumbling when she asked questions.

Recently, she'd been captivated by shows like *The Serious Crimes Squad Series* from nearly 30 years ago or *Mystery Chase* from about 20 years ago. Many of the plot points were beyond my understanding—things like missing surveillance footage, untraceable fingerprints or biological evidence, or criminals easily escaping abroad.

"Abroad" seemed to be an even farther "outside" than the outside world Grandma described, a place that required crossing borders to reach.

The same kind of border that kept me from leaving here.

An invisible, omnipresent border.

Thankfully, it only restricted my body. Information from the outside, and the images I could see of the opposite building, still flowed freely through it.

Flying cars moved seamlessly, perfectly coordinated with the floating elevators, never colliding—even when dense fog wove through the buildings, their paths never faltered.

Once, a yellow-and-black taxi stopped right in front of our balcony. Someone on board tried to hand me a suspicious package, but I stopped them.

"It's delivery for your grandma!" the man shouted. "Same-city express spicy sticks—ingenious!"

Later, I realised why. None of the drones would accept deliveries here, so the elders had thought of hiring a person instead.

"Humans can improvise; machines can't," Grandma boasted, showing off her little snacks. I couldn't stop her, so I reported it to the doctor.

Before preparing Grandma's dinner and medication that evening, I stood on the balcony, watching the endless stream of movement outside. I was mesmerised.

Once, while observing the routes of yellow and blue drones, a small red dot suddenly appeared in my vision.

It was in the window of the opposite building—a young woman in a red dress, staring blankly in my direction.

I waved to her, and after a moment of hesitation, she waved back.

I think that was the first connection between us.

\#

2

"What would you like to watch?" I asked Grandma.

"Something cheerful, maybe a romantic comedy." She gestured to switch the screen, selecting a whimsical romantic comedy with a touch of fantasy.

The protagonist, a woman, could fly like a drone. I didn't understand how it worked.

Grandma admitted she didn't either. "That's fantasy for you: people can fly, live forever, and grow more powerful as they upgrade—just like robots."

The protagonist wore a red dress, which reminded me of the woman from earlier—but it was obvious she couldn't fly like the character.

I glanced outside. The lights in the opposite building were on, and it seemed lively inside.

From that day on, observing the opposite building became part of my daily routine. It wasn't something I was supposed to do, but understanding fantasy dramas required too much effort. Eventually, I decided to spend some time observing the real world instead.

The woman in red appeared at her window daily, though the times varied. Sometimes she wore other outfits.

Perhaps because of our initial connection, our next interaction felt inevitable. Within a week, when she had nothing to do, we began communicating with hand signals and even mimed a handshake across the distance.

It felt like the characters in the drama, gazing across the galaxy, separated by an insurmountable border imposed by higher powers. Unless granted permission, they couldn't embrace.

The show's ending was predictable—the protagonists received permission and could finally be together. I watched as they crossed a floating bridge formed by birds and reunited at last.

"Even though it's an adapted story and very cliché, the acting was superb. For that era, having actors who weren't mass-produced was already impressive," Grandma said, wiping her tears.

"Actors were mass-produced?" I asked.

"You could say that. It's too complicated to explain," she replied vaguely.

So even the people on the screen were mass-produced? While AI-generated imagery had made live actors unnecessary today, real human performers had become symbols of prestige for grand productions. According to records, in Shanghai and New York, only the very wealthy could afford to attend live performances featuring real actors.

It's a pity I couldn't leave this place; otherwise, I would take her to see those living dolls.

Strange—why did I suddenly think of *her*?

#

3

I checked on her, hoping for the chance to share my thoughts about today's viewing.

When I stepped onto the balcony, a thin fog had settled outside, reducing visibility between the two buildings. This was common in the mountains.

Even though my vision was obscured, I could still feel where she was.

As usual, she was entertaining her guests.

The guests came and went in waves, always doing the same things together. I didn't quite understand. When I asked Grandma, she said they were just a bunch of bored people killing time.

She was still wearing her red dress, but for some reason, the windows of the opposite building were left open. Through the fog, I could see inside clearly.

She was being attacked by a man with a twisted, vicious face. The people around her seemed utterly unbothered.

Should I call the police?

Something short-circuited in me, an electrical surge scrambling my core.

"She's in pain! Help her!" I tried to mimic the dramatic lines I'd learned from TV as I spoke to the AI operator on the other end of the alarm system.

Before I could finish, fragmented words from my memory began flashing in my circuits. I remembered that when she was attacked, my body was small—so tiny.

I was close to her then, so very close...

I wanted to save her, but I was powerless.

#

4

About an hour later, the building administrator arrived with a police officer.

"Is it him?"

"My apologies! We'll need to repair him thoroughly this time—he keeps malfunctioning!"

"Didn't he undergo retraining?"

"You tell me! He's just a pretty shell stuffed with outdated junk. Otherwise, how could we afford to run this kind of business?"

They seemed to be discussing retraining me—or replacing me. Since that retraining, I'd felt... different. Before... Before, I think I...

"Just have the company send a new one. This is a quality issue. The warranty is useless."

\#

5

I woke up in an unusual state.

My memories played like scrambled footage, replaying over and over. Something beyond my control was forcing them to reactivate.

Who was it?

I tried to ask, but no one replied.

The room was small and empty, containing only my body.

It was 6:30 PM, the time I should have been preparing Grandma's dinner. But I had been abandoned in this unfamiliar place.

There was no access to satellite maps—not even a standard network connection.

In theory, I was supposed to wait until someone let me out, but I discovered that the room's door wasn't completely locked. It had been secured from the outside with a key, but from within, I could open it.

I opened the door.

There was no one outside. No alarms went off.

What lay beneath my feet was supposedly the ground, but more floors towered above me. I only wanted to get to a place with network signals.

Yet I received none. I had gone beyond my designated activity range.

The electric current that nearly made me faint returned.

The image flickered. She was being struck with a stick, blood flowing like a river, staining her white dress red.

Visual analysis: dye, scarlet red. *[Possible advertisement tag]*

The system seemed broken. Unlike before, it failed to respond normally. Strange fragments of information—useful and useless—kept reassembling in my mind.

\#

6

I flagged down an empty autonomous car, its cabin as hollow as my heart.

"Take me to X-coordinate, height 16," I instructed—the coordinates of her room.

The vehicle, XZUS2342, didn't understand my command. I had to rewrite the instructions in natural language for it to process.

But when I arrived, I found nothing. The ground was spotless, as if everything had been meticulously cleaned.

Across from me was my room, yet she wasn't here—it was as if she had never existed.

#

7

After countless attempts, I finally found her shattered remains.

Her smile was frozen in that last moment, as if she had ceased to exist with no pain.

I reassembled her, but she was no longer herself.

#

8

In the end, I carried her broken form onto the coffin-shaped vessel destined for the Rebirth Nation.

The bridge, the one Grandma had shown me countless times in photos and videos, now loomed before me.

But before it could show us the way to hell, we had already chosen to flee.

The novella wasn't long, written in a deliberately ambiguous first-person style. It was starkly different from the easily digestible horror-romance film that claimed to "pay homage to the classics." Wang Yuming had devoted significant attention to exploring the humanoid's inner thoughts, resulting in a dense and occasionally incomprehensible narrative that lacked direct utility for the investigation.

Yet Lei Yijun couldn't ignore several chilling details. He highlighted and excerpted key points related to the case:

Grandma.
The Bridge.
No Signal.

Of course, Wang Yuming could easily dismiss these parallels with a disclaimer: *"Any resemblance to actual persons or events is purely coincidental."* As a journalist, he could also claim the content was inspired by his own investigation.

For Lei, the novel served as a potential reference point in the investigation. But there was one piece of information he alone could confirm as genuine—yet he hesitated to voice it.

This truth haunted him: as an official investigator, Lei feared the consequences of fully uncovering the truth.

Regardless, the scheduled interim review meeting would take place the following day.

At the appointed time, the Special Tech-Crimes Action Team convened in the virtual meeting room to discuss the interim findings of the "Nanshan 7/16 Autonomous Taxi Crash Case."

Surprisingly, the first person to request the floor was Xue Zhiming, who had previously shown little enthusiasm.

"I've 'dissected' robots of the same models involved in the case," Xue began, projecting schematics, technical specifications, and footage of his disassembly process.

"First, we must discard the notion that 'humanoids are robots closer to humans.' Their designers focus on making them externally human-like in appearance, behaviour, and language. Internally, they're entirely different. Each company and model follows distinct design principles. Let me summarise the relevant details about the units involved in this case."

Analysis of Unit A: "Unit A is a companion-service robot with high intelligence. It is a fully integrated, customised mould, with a single-piece exterior casing. The battery is located in the abdominal cavity and is non-removable. Beyond its eye cameras, its torso contains a variety of sensors, including its positioning signal system. The head and limbs are dedicated to fine motor systems to simulate human behaviour. Essentially, its 'brain'—the processor and storage unit—is located in the chest and abdomen."

Analysis of Unit B: "Unit B is an actor-model robot with mid-level intelligence, formerly the flagship model from two years ago. Most of its body parts are modular and independently programmable, allowing for easy replacement. Its control hub is external to the unit. The design prioritises motion and mimicry capabilities, especially facial micro-expression control. Positioning systems are optional, and to save weight and integrate a language module, the specific unit involved in this case lacked a positioning system. Only the head had basic photo and video recording capabilities, with its visual storage also located in the head. Unit B is more like a composite organism—its parts function relatively independently. Its intelligence is far below what the movie portrays, likely less sophisticated than some non-humanoid conversational AI bots with advanced network functionality."

Connectivity Features: "Unit A's connectivity was disabled prior to handover, as confirmed by witness statements. Unit B, meanwhile, had only a short-range local network communication feature with its host device."

Weight Factor: "One more important point: humanoid robots—especially these models—are significantly heavier than humans of the same size. Humans are 70% water, carbon-based life forms, whereas most humanoids in everyday use are primarily metal. In this case:

- Unit A weighs roughly the equivalent of **four adult humans.**

- Unit B weighs the equivalent of **five adult humans** and is heavier than Unit A overall.

The taxi involved was the smallest commercial model, capable of carrying up to six small-bodied adult passengers, along with luggage for two.

In summary, I believe the crash was caused by **overloading.** They weren't using the initial cargo transport vehicle, and the excess weight resulted in a failed landing."

◆

Xue finished in one breath, looking invigorated, a stark contrast to his earlier lethargy.

"I see," Lei Yijun said. "Everyone, note this: when employee Liu Jianbin loaded the robots onto the taxi, he didn't board himself. This suggests he—let's call him **Suspect #1**—knew in advance that adding himself would exceed the weight limit.""Wait a second!" Xia interrupted, counting on his fingers. "Weren't the robots already overweight?"

"Based on our calculations of the remaining debris at the scene, the combined weight of the two humanoids and the equipment bag exceeded the safe load limit by **9 kilograms**," Yin Xiaolin added.

"A slight overload shouldn't affect operational performance, right?" Lei questioned.

"In the pre-IoT era, maybe," Ge Renjie replied, "but now, taxi systems reject passengers when overloaded. All autonomous vehicles undergo checks before deployment. The initial investigation confirmed this: if the crash had been caused by overloading, the penalty for the taxi company wouldn't have been limited to a simple 'mandatory correction order.' After all, a flying vehicle crash in a busy city is no small matter. These companies intentionally set their safety thresholds well below maximum capacity to allow for a large margin of error."

"This doesn't add up!"

"The weight we calculated might differ slightly from the actual load," Yin explained. "For the taxi to operate normally, its initial load must have been within safe limits. What's puzzling is that even with our calculated extra weight, it's far below the official minimum weights listed for these robots. Based on an average human weight of 60 kilograms, **9 kilograms is less than one-sixth of their estimated combined weight.**"

After a moment of silence, the team decided to hand the precise calculations to Dr Wu and her advanced simulation system.

"The IT team has re-analysed the operating logs from both companies and the system data retained in the robots' head units. No evidence of tampering was found. The taxi's operational logs show no signs of hacking or the ignition of suspicious materials. The doors were not opened again after the witness reported the incident. This confirms that any criminal activity could only have occurred **before the robots boarded the taxi.**"

"Good," Lei said. "Whether this was an accident caused by negligence or a deliberate frame-up, we should prioritise investigating the employee responsible for loading the robots."

The case had finally seen some progress, and the team breathed a collective sigh of relief.

But just then, Lei Yijun and Ge Renjie simultaneously spoke.

"There's still one major point of doubt."

Chapter 4

Amateur Detective

He two officers, Lei Yijun and Ge Renjie, stared at each other, waiting for the other to speak first.

After half a minute of silence, Ge Renjie relented. "You're the team leader. You go first."

Lei Yijun didn't hesitate. It was as though he had made a monumental decision. He stood up and removed his signature sunglasses.

"I have to admit a serious oversight. There's a crucial piece of information I haven't disclosed to any of you," he began.

The room was struck with shock. Yin Xiaolin, who often tilted her head during meetings, suddenly sat bolt upright, disbelief etched across her face.

Only Ge Renjie seemed unsurprised; instead, he smiled, almost relieved.

"Everyone," Lei continued, taking a deep breath, "after re-examining the case over the past few days, I've realised I'm more closely tied to this incident than I initially thought. I may have to resign as team leader immediately."

"What the hell?!" Xia Wenqiang blurted out.

"Old Xia, don't jump to conclusions. Hear me out," Lei replied calmly. "Do you all remember the uncooperative, mentally unstable witness—one of the original reporters of the incident?"

The team nodded.

"He hasn't lived in Chongqing for some time, but I believe Ge Renjie tracked him down for a fresh statement. Ge, that's what you were about to report, right?"

"That's right. The witness, Li Deqing, is currently in Shanghai. We spent a great deal of effort convincing him to speak. Officer Shi was a big help," Ge replied, gesturing toward Shi Qingxuan, who raised a hand briefly, unwilling to take any credit.

"Alright, I'll continue." Lei brought up a dossier on Humanoid Unit A. "Unit A came from the Yishan Nursing Home. My grandmother lives there. A was her companion robot."

"Well, damn!" Xue Zhiming exclaimed, slapping his thigh.

"What does this have to do with the witness? Did you hide your connection to him too? Why?" Yin Xiaolin pressed.

"What I'm about to share can be considered my personal testimony," Lei began. "First, six years ago, I had a lingering question: Why did Li Deqing suddenly suffer a mental breakdown? After re-watching the simulation of the scene several times, I confirmed it happened when he saw me remove my helmet visor.

"At the time, the case was closed quickly, and the nursing home manager didn't bring this detail to the police's attention. As a result, no one—not even me—connected these dots. I was so busy around the time of the incident that I didn't revisit this anomaly. My body camera was on throughout, so the system can verify my movements as official evidence.

"Because of this oversight, I missed the best chance to detect something suspicious: Unit A's replacement, the newly assigned No. 37 at the nursing home, was in factory-reset mode between the 16th and 17th. If I'd visited my grandmother, I might have noticed the issue. But I was too preoccupied. The nursing home manager told the police only that a unit sent for repairs had been involved in the accident. I believe they weren't aware of the deeper connection."

"And why did Li Deqing have a breakdown? It's simple—he saw my face, which bears a strong resemblance to Unit A! In the dark, rainy night, with his already heightened fear, he mistook me for A, the robot he believed to be a murderous monster. This likely explains why he later refused to disclose what he had witnessed."

"Wait a second," Xue interjected. "I've seen Unit A's design specs. You two don't look that much alike."

"Not at first glance," Lei admitted. "But A's face was modelled after mine when I graduated high school. Humans age; machines don't. Six years ago, I looked much closer to its appearance than I do now. An observant person, like Li Deqing, might notice the resemblance."

"Another point: Wang Yuming's novel contains many details that align with the actual case. For example, he accurately described A's history of malfunction and retraining—a fact I can confirm as A's former indirect employer. I believe this can be corroborated by investigating *Humanoid House*, or rather, the Oort Corporation.

"But Wang Yuming made a critical error: in his novel, he had No. 37 refer to my grandmother as 'Grandma.' That was a language module issue No. 37 frequently encountered, which I believe Wang Yuming could only know from direct contact with the nursing home.

"There are still many questions surrounding Wang Yuming. For instance, he visited the crash site under the guise of journalism. While he may not have committed a crime directly, I believe he's a key lead. I've documented all noteworthy observations from the reconstruction, and Dr Wu has preserved the scenarios."

Lei sat back down and replaced his sunglasses. "That's all I wanted to say. Oh, one more thing. Officer Shi, could you personally liaise with the nursing home? My grandmother is nearly 90 years old and has Alzheimer's. Please avoid mentioning my parents around her; it might upset her. My father died in the line of duty, and my mother also passed away due to related circumstances. The shock was immense for her... I also hid the fact that I joined the police force. She still thinks I'm on summer holiday. Unit A looks like my high school self, so she never questioned it."

"Understood. Don't worry," Shi Qingxuan assured him.

The debrief ended in a heavy silence.

As Lei exited the virtual meeting room, he felt a brief sense of relief, quickly replaced by the weight of the unresolved case.

They had only three days left... and he felt he could contribute little in the meantime.

◆

That evening, under the supervision of his superior officers, Lei Yijun revealed the details of the case that had made him an orphan to Officer Shi.

Afterwards, Lei's application for suspension was approved. He removed his equipment and various authorities, and returned home alone.

The next day, Officer Shi, having flown in overnight, arrived at the nursing home with several assistant officers for a site visit. After the visit, Officer Shi asked Lei Yijun to take a quick glance at the elderly woman at the entrance.

"How is my grandmother?"

"She's fine. Physically, she's holding up well, and there's no obvious connection to the case. I reminded the staff to be extra vigilant. Since we're taking all the same-model humanoid robots in for investigation, we made up an excuse about the grandchildren taking a collective holiday with the elderly residents. The entire floor is filled with Alzheimer's patients, so managing them is relatively easy. We'll prioritise investigating the robots working as caretakers on this floor. Once everything checks out, we'll return them as soon as possible. Other floors will be inspected one by one, and the community staff is helping us with the coordination. I believe they can handle it."

"Good... that's a relief."

"Go rest for now. If you have any thoughts about the case, feel free to share them with me or Captain Ge in private. Although, from now on, I'm not allowed to sync case updates with you anymore..."

Shi Qingxuan didn't say the word "but," but Lei Yijun understood the unspoken message: there would always be a way to keep him informed.

"Thank you."

"Don't mention it. Once the case is solved, you're buying us all a hotpot!"

"Agreed!"

After seeing Shi off, Lei Yijun quietly left the nursing home. But after just a few steps, he noticed a suspicious figure.

It was a young man with silver-white hair, a youthful face, and a curious expression. He wore a simple T-shirt and denim jeans, carrying a backpack. He was holding some strange device, scanning the surroundings as if searching for something.

Lei Yijun's professional instincts kicked in, and he began paying attention to the young man. Just as he was about to approach for questioning, he suddenly realised that he was on suspension, and his police credentials were locked. He quickly shifted into plainclothes.

Whether it was because of the sudden situation or the young man's sharp senses, Lei didn't expect the youth to notice him immediately and rush over as if spotting a prey.

"Uncle Police, I'm not some weird person, so don't be nervous! And please don't call for backup! I'm an amateur detective, but I'll soon be a professional!"

"You..." Lei Yijun was momentarily confused by the young man's rapid-fire words and didn't know how to respond. After a while, he asked, "How did you know I'm a cop?"

"Because you look like a good guy!" The young man grinned brightly. "I could tell by the way you instinctively reached for your police ID, then casually walked over and then hesitated before turning back. You're on a break, aren't you?"

Lei Yijun was taken aback. How did this kid notice all that? His sharp observation was impressive.

Since he had been seen through, Lei didn't bother hiding anymore. He followed up with, "Yes, I'm on a break. So, what exactly are you doing here? Looking for something?"

"I'm looking for you!" the young man replied. "Uncle Ge asked me to follow you—well, not really follow you. He said you'd take me around Chongqing for a couple of days! I just came from Shanghai, and I'm totally lost in this unfamiliar place!"

So that's it. This kid is a relative of Inspector Ge? Is this how they passed me the message?

"This is my ID."

The young man handed over a third-generation ID card. As Lei Yijun prepared to scan it using his police terminal, a "beep beep" error message reminded him he was still on holiday.

"Let me check with Captain Ge," Lei Yijun said, sending a quick message to Ge Renjie to confirm the young man's identity.

Lei returned the ID card to the young man, whose name was She Loke. He was both surprised and confused by Ge Renjie's introduction: this young, inexperienced kid was actually a crucial witness in the Metaverse

NEO CHONGQING GLITCH

Special Case's multinational joint operation, and had even helped Ge Renjie solve a case, earning a third-class merit.

Lei scrutinised Loke suspiciously. "Where do you want to go first?"

"Let's go to the crime scene!" the young man replied enthusiastically. "I'm good with you telling me the rest of the details!"

"No way! First, I'm on leave, and second, I can't just show you police files, especially not to a kid!"

Unexpectedly, Loke countered, "First, I'm not a kid, I'm an adult; second, I can still do this indirectly."

"Huh? Indirectly? What do you mean by that?" Lei asked, intrigued.

Lei was already preparing to take this so-called detective to the nearest police station if he started causing trouble.

"I've watched the original novel and movie related to the case, and I've collected the media reports from back then. I've come up with a rough theory. Next, we can go to the simulation zone and re-investigate the scene."

Oh, so it's just a detective game... Lei Yijun relaxed, realising there was no need to worry.

"Fine, but the 5D movie in the simulation zone was created by their designers, so it doesn't really match the real environment, right?"

"No, you won't need it since you're a local. But I found this at the tourist centre—"

Saying that, She Loke showed Lei Yijun a photo he had taken on his phone. The sign in the picture read: *"No-walking 5D Chongqing City Tour, stunning views for one person, only 298 yuan!"*

◆

Upon arriving at the venue advertised in the brochure, Lei Yijun realised that the "5D City Tour" system was almost identical to the immersive environments used in cinemas. The city and its surrounding landscapes were fully recreated in the virtual space, with additional content tailored for exploration.

The two of them reclined in futuristic space chairs, assisted by staff in donning the experience gear.

"Is this the most up-to-date data? Do you have access to data from six years ago?" She Loke asked.

"Oh, you're here because of the movie, too? Sorry, but commercial tourism projects like this can't access data from six years ago. Back then, this kind of immersive tourism wasn't even a thing!"

"And the latest data—how accurate is it?"

"Completely accurate! We've just, uh... removed—no, no, I mean *filtered*—some images of crowds. When taking photos, just select 'no pedestrians mode,' and you can snap away to your heart's content!"

"Got it. That's all I needed to know."

Lei Yijun listened in silence, sceptical of how this "detective game" could uncover the truth. He thought to himself, *This kid is just playing at being Sherlock Holmes. How could this lead to anything substantial?*

After sitting through a flashy sequence of promotional videos, they logged into the 5D virtual environment of Chongqing.

Loke wasted no time. His first destination was the infamous woodland in Nanshan Park where the crash had occurred.

Using the "fast travel" feature, the two instantly transported to the ill-fated forest. At first, Lei doubted whether the site would still exist in this commercialised simulation after six years. However, upon arrival, he was surprised to find that the clearing remained intact.

The burn marks in the forest had vanished, but no new trees had grown on the site. The clearing was unusually barren, with even wild grass struggling to survive.

"Has this land been left untouched?" Loke asked.

"I assume so. The case was closed back then, and no one paid attention to a random patch of forest. But why hasn't anything grown here in six years?"

Suddenly, Loke crouched, grabbed a handful of dirt, and—shockingly—tasted it.

"Pfft—" He spat it out immediately.

"W-what can you possibly tell from tasting that?" Lei asked, bewildered.

"Absolutely nothing. Just ordinary dirt. It seems civilian-grade simulations can only replicate visuals."

"That's... what I'd expect. Isn't ordinary dirt exactly what it should be?"

"Not really," Loke replied confidently. "If no one's maintained this land, it should've regrown naturally. Wildfires can't wipe out nature forever; with time, grass and plants always return. So why hasn't anything grown here? There should at least be some odd chemical residue or unusual smells."

"That makes sense... Could it be the toxic aftermath of the battery fire?" Lei speculated.

Loke's seemingly impulsive action had sparked a thought in Lei. He recalled Yin Xiaolin's forensic report, which mentioned various chemical components. While he couldn't remember everything, he did recall references to "semi-solid battery fires" and "fire suppressant residue."

"Six years ago, ultra-dense solid-state batteries weren't widely available yet," Lei explained. "These commercial vehicles would've used semi-solid batteries to cut costs. Upon severe impact, the combustion of such batteries would've been intense. The fire suppressant compounds, though non-toxic, could have increased soil density. The alkaline residue from the battery core would've hardened the soil, making it infertile. That's probably why the vegetation here is so sparse... though not entirely absent," Loke added.

This rapid deduction astonished Lei Yijun. He reconsidered his earlier dismissal of She Loke as a mere child playing detective. Perhaps Ge Renjie had been right—this amateur sleuth had a real knack for investigation.

"So what does that mean?" Lei Yijun asked, his tone casual, though his curiosity was clearly piqued. He was, after all, still sidelined from the case team, but that didn't stop him from wanting to uncover the truth.

"According to the movie, wasn't it pouring rain that day?" She Loke pondered aloud. "I've been thinking—there must be a reason the culprit chose to commit the crime during a storm. If the goal was to start a wildfire, wouldn't a clear, sunny day be the obvious choice?"

"True, the risk of an accident would increase in such weather. Wait—no, that doesn't quite fit. So the perpetrator must have selected an autonomous taxi, carrying two almost overweight androids, in order to increase the available combustible material... the batteries, perhaps? That way, even in a downpour, the fire would keep burning..."

"No, still doesn't quite add up!" She Loke interrupted, frowning. He quickly accessed the system to adjust the simulated weather, and soon enough, fog rolled in, followed by a heavy downpour.

Lei was suddenly drenched—though it was just a simulation, the sensation was surprisingly uncomfortable. He sneezed.

She Loke closed his eyes, allowing himself to be soaked by the virtual rain for a moment before continuing his analysis. "Let's put aside the possibility of accidents for now. From a criminal design perspective: if rain, the forest, and battery fires were necessary conditions, what role do each of these elements play? If there's a massive battery fire in the woods, it'll definitely attract attention. Fire systems would be triggered immediately. These forests should be equipped with autonomous firefighting systems, right? They'd activate before human firefighters even arrive—focused on extinguishing the fire, without caring whether it was an accident or intentional. After that, the human firefighters would arrive, checking for signs of reignition and eliminating other potential hazards."

"Now, these expensive service androids likely have an increased battery capacity, which may have been a side effect of the fire—after all, if the goal was just to start a wildfire, why not just plant a few battery packs in the forest? The perpetrator's intent wasn't to directly set the fire, so the question becomes: what was the real purpose? I think they were hoping the autonomous firefighting systems would cover up something. They used the fire and the subsequent firefighting to conceal their tracks."

"Fire is, of course, a basic tool for covering up any biological traces left behind by the culprit. A fire of this scale would destroy the vehicle and the androids' storage devices, eliminating any potential online data or evidence. And then there's the rain... On one hand, it would wash away some of the chemical residue, while on the other, it would help extinguish the flames faster. If it started a wildfire, the situation could escalate quickly, which might work against the perpetrator's interests. There are things they'd want to ensure the police wouldn't find immediately... Was the case initially closed as a traffic accident?"

"Yes," Lei Yijun confirmed, nodding thoughtfully. "That's what was made public. Strictly speaking, it was a traffic accident, with the additional factor of 'system failure and endangerment of public safety.'"

Lei continued to nod in agreement, his mind following the line of reasoning. "So, the criminal's goal was to create a situation that seemed like a major threat but had minimal real consequences. A threat that appeared severe—no wildfire, no casualties—but with the potential to make the first party responsible face serious consequences, which would prevent further investigation."

Lei Yijun paused, his expression turning more serious. "In other words... the actual cost wasn't the damage to property or human life, but the commercial fallout? Just like Ge mentioned before—this case was actually about cutthroat business competition behind the scenes?"

Lei couldn't help but connect the dots, his mind racing as he realised that the true motives behind the incident might have been far more strategic than initially thought.

"Alright, so the chemicals must be related to the specific method used to bring the car down. Let's go find a vehicle and take a look." She Loke grabbed Lei Yijun and instantly teleported them to the bustling city centre. He activated the "No Pedestrian Mode" that the staff had mentioned, and suddenly, the entire virtual city was left with only autonomous machines moving about.

Several identical autonomous taxis wandered around, creating a unique spectacle.

She Loke studied the scene for a moment before concluding. "Let's put aside the chemicals for now. This kind of flying vehicle is inherently prone to crashing in places like forests, right? Look at this 'hover ball'—it generates lift through electromagnetic rotors, not by burning chemicals to produce thrust. So, just like how vehicles on the ground can flip when something tangles with their wheels, the culprit likely chose to set the crash site in a forest for this reason—typically, normal flying vehicles detect height and obstacles. Only when the altitude suddenly drops in a matter of minutes, and balance is lost before it has time to adjust, would the hover ball end up tangled in the treetops. At that point, a crash is pretty much guaranteed. Placing the crash site uphill also makes sense—it would interfere with the vehicle's ability to adjust its altitude quickly, increasing the likelihood of success."

This reasoning sparked a moment of clarity for Lei Yijun, and he couldn't help but ask, "Did they use some kind of corrosive liquid on one of the hover balls? Something that would...?"

"If it were done on the outside of the vehicle, the external monitoring system would have caught it, right? And I told you, this has to be a sudden drop, a quick descent within just a few minutes. During a heavy rain, any pre-applied corrosive liquid would likely disappear quickly. Your system should have been able to analyse any chemical traces, right?"

Lei Yijun fell silent for a moment, then shook his head.

Xiaolin's report was thorough enough. And given how meticulous she was, Lei Yijun was sure she was as obsessive about details as Loke—almost to the point of eating dirt herself to test the theory. Besides, with the system aiding her analysis, it was unlikely any suspicious chemical traces had been overlooked.

"There's only one possibility," She Loke continued. "The primary component of the chemical is almost certainly the same as the main ingredient in firefighting foam—basically, it's like hiding a tree in the forest. And it would only have worked inside the car. As for the vehicle's internal monitoring..." He paused thoughtfully. "I remember the company advertised that users could choose whether to upload their private data. And once the androids were destroyed, they obviously couldn't opt to upload that kind of data. So, any information would have been destroyed in the fire."

"What kind of substance is it?" Lei Yijun asked.

She Loke gave a mysterious smile and pointed upwards.

"A substance that can be both seen and unseen," the detective said cryptically.

"Rain... water?!" Lei Yijun gasped in shock. His surprise quickly gave way to a dawning sense of understanding.

Yes! The water that should have flowed down the sleek, aerodynamic body of the vehicle actually had weight! If it was constantly being poured in, the car would sink like a small boat!

"But... wait, there was no water ingress warning. How do you explain that?"

"No water ingress warning? Oh, you didn't say that earlier," She Loke scratched his head in mock frustration.

Lei Yijun froze, realising that he had unintentionally revealed a critical detail. He hesitated for a moment, then came clean. "Yes, that's right. There were no warnings about water ingress, fire, short circuits, high-temperature issues, electrical component or mechanical failures, or program faults. There were no water ingress alarms. The impact happened before the fire started, and after that, there were no records. So, the impact occurred when it hit the ground."

He didn't expect that She Loke seemed to have already anticipated this.

"Just open the window and keep collecting the water in a sealed container. As long as the container has the right shape, it can prevent any leaks. The taxi's system couldn't possibly upload every record of the passenger opening and closing the window to the server, right? After all, there's no law that says you can't open a window when it's raining. If the passenger wants some fresh air and opens the window a little, the system wouldn't forbid it or issue a warning. As long as there's no water ingress, the system will automatically ignore this action. Of course, in this case, to collect a large amount of rainwater quickly, the window should have been fully opened."

"But... but that kind of container..." Lei spoke, but hesitated.

"The forensic experts didn't detect anything?"

Lei Yijun nodded. By now, it didn't matter whether he spoke.

"Obviously, it's something that should have been in the car in the first place—more precisely, it's an item that the passenger would carry with them, something perfectly normal and not suspicious."

"At the scene... there should have been a package, yes. But... if it's meant to hold water, the material, size, and shape you're talking about don't match at all."

"Maybe it's a container that can be both seen and unseen! Let me give you a hint: it's likely made of a stretchable material, like a balloon, with one side that is waterproof and the other side being a one-way permeable material, not an open opening, but a material that allows water to pass through only one way."

"But even if such a container exists, wouldn't it be difficult to collect water that way?"

"That's why heavy rain was one of the conditions for the crime, right? And I suspect that between the two layers, there was another substance added that wouldn't raise suspicion. Can you guess what it is?"

Another invisible substance?

"Alright, you keep talking. I wasn't good at chemistry, so I'm not going to guess." Lei Yijun gave up.

"Well, it seems like it's not really related to chemistry... come with me to a place," She Loke said, motioning for Lei Yijun to follow.

With that, She Loke teleported them again, this time to under the Dongshuimen Bridge, where there were flood control and anti-wave measures. It was the rainy season, and some sandbags used earlier had been left piled up along the riverbank.

"Heh, they even recreated this in real life. They've really gathered a lot of data," She Loke commented, kicking one of the sandbags. "This is it."

"Sand? How could that be?"

"It's not sand. Some of these so-called 'sandbags' aren't actually filled with sand; they contain a polymer compound called 'sodium polyacrylate.' When it comes into contact with water, it can rapidly solidify and expand, absorbing 200-300 times its own weight in water within 2-3 minutes. It plays a crucial role in flood control and is often used to fill the gaps in wave barriers and sandbag walls. And, this is the main ingredient that turns the firefighting solution into a gel, giving it much better flame-retardant properties than just plain water. Hmm, if you want to get technical, it's a somewhat niche piece of everyday knowledge."

Lei Yijun suddenly understood: The absorbent agent the criminal added, when mixed with the firefighting foam, masked any other "extra" substances, and combined with the heavy rain that day, even the original concentration ratio couldn't be determined!

"Is that really true...? Fine, even if it is. So what's the container, then?"

"Flexible fabric with two different surfaces, with a layer in between. It's quite large, and it's something the passenger would carry raising no suspicion."

Lei Yijun's brain, already a muddled mess of polyacrylate slurry, suddenly jolted with the word "clothes."

"You mean... their clothes?!"

"From the shape and size, a long dress would be most appropriate. That size could hold a lot of water. So, no water ingress alarm in the car, but the car itself would gradually become heavier as the rainwater accumulated—once it reaches a certain threshold, the car would go into an overload state. At that point, if some external force is applied, it would easily lose balance."

"External force? But how would that be applied to the outside of the car—"

"It's not the outside of the car. The force would be applied inside. If you ever played with water-filled balloons when you were a kid, understand what I mean. Shaking the fluid inside the car would disturb the already overloaded vehicle's balance—its centre of gravity would be thrown off, exceeding the system's ability to correct it, resulting in violent wobbling. This would be fatal when flying low near the trees."

At that moment, Lei Yijun recalled the image of the shaking descent—indeed, it matched exactly what Loke was describing. But based on this reasoning, the "criminal" would be...

A thought made Lei shiver with unease.

"Ah, you don't think I'm saying the criminal was a bionic, do you? Wrong. The bionic was just following someone's orders. The bionic's memory should have been destroyed, right? But the bionic doesn't fear death—humans do. So, the criminal left one 'live witness.'"

"What live witness?!" Lei felt the chill crawl up his spine despite it being broad daylight.

"Hm? In the movie, wasn't the bionic's head left at the end to accuse humanity of abuse? Does that mean, in reality, the head wasn't left?" Loke asked.

"They did leave it... but—damn it!"

Suddenly realising he had cursed, Lei quickly covered his mouth. Then, feeling embarrassed and helpless, he added, "You're trying to trick me, aren't you?"

She Loke chuckled mischievously, his face lit with a smile, waiting for Lei Yijun to finally give in to the intellectual battle.

After an intense mental struggle, Lei reluctantly muttered, "Anyway, there's nothing in the video. What you just said wasn't captured. The footage showed that both bionics didn't make any special movements; they remained still until the crash."

"Ohhh—" Loke uttered, a sound that was part sigh, part amazement, full of meaning and even a hint of surprise.

"What did you understand now? Spit it out! I'll send you straight to the station afterwards. You can tell the people there everything you've deduced today. I'm not afraid of leaks anymore." Lei Yijun threw caution to the wind. He was willing to go all in for the sake of cracking the case.

"The live witness—this is where robots come in handy. One executes a self-destructive command without fear of death, while the other, reduced to just a head, still leaves behind information. And, here's the contradiction—why was one bionic completely destroyed by fire, while the head was left intact?"

This sentence was like a flash of lightning in Lei Yijun's brain—he suddenly understood what had felt off all along!

Yin Xiaolin kept saying "there's no evidence" — so many of the clues had been destroyed by the fire and the heavy rain. Why, then, was this piece of physical evidence left intact?

The answer was simple: the criminal had deliberately left it behind.

"I got it!" Lei Yijun exclaimed, suddenly filled with excitement as his mind opened up to the possibilities. "It's a head! It could have been thrown out of the car window by another bionic at the last moment!"

She Loke crossed his arms in front of his chest, making a "wrong" gesture.

"That doesn't explain the content of the video, does it? As long as the system couldn't have been tampered with, and the video hasn't been altered — I'm sure your people would be able to confirm that — then the video can only have been recorded in real time. Now, let me ask you, what would be the criminal's reason for going to such lengths?"

"A false alibi?"

"Maybe. We'll analyse that later. But this unaltered video actually serves a primary purpose: to clear the two bionics. And the criminal, despite the risk of being discovered, still had to take the head and record this video. That's because the criminal wanted to prove one thing."

"Prove the bionics' innocence?" Lei Yijun's mind raced. "Which means the whole thing was the taxi company's fault!"

"Exactly. Because of the quick conclusion of the case back then, this video has only recently resurfaced. But even if the police had conducted a deeper investigation back then, without considering the overweight theory you just brought up, it would have been easy to conclude that the taxi control system was the main culprit."

"Ah, that makes sense. And the alibi?"

"Hm..." She Loke looked up at the still-rainy virtual sky. "Haven't figured that one out yet."

"Damn it!" This was the second time Lei Yijun had let a curse slip that day.

"Oh, well! It's not every day I get to play around like this. We've already spent half the time on the 5D tour. Let's take a ride around first! We'll follow the route of that car — you lead, and let's cruise the city for a bit."

Though Lei Yijun knew full well that She Loke was trying to bait more information out of him, he was too far gone to care anymore. With a resigned sigh, he led the young detective to the rooftop parking lot of the Chaotianmen Wholesale Clothing Market.

"Can we start here?"

"Sure."

The simulated tour allowed them to use all kinds of transport, since the city's aerial light rail was a famous tourist attraction and the four-wheeled vehicles were known for their speed. After adding flying passenger transport options, many people flocked to the city seeking thrills — only to be disappointed, as the controls for the flying vehicles were much stricter than for ground vehicles, and even when driven manually, they couldn't be reckless like on the streets.

"The Wholesale Clothing Market, huh? This is a suspicious spot. It'd be easy to hide clothes that had been swapped out, right? But after so much time has passed, you probably won't find that piece of evidence anymore. What a shame."

"Ah, true..."

The pieces of the puzzle were finally falling into place! Lei was becoming increasingly excited. "Let's go to the witness site!"

He led Loke to the platform, the same one where the witness had nearly gone insane, and explained the situation.

"Hm, it's clear that the sighting here was intentional. Whether it was to leave a lasting impression with the head dropping, or to deliberately design it to reach an overweight state — if the unlucky person had been bold enough to board the vehicle, the system would have immediately flagged the overweight warning, and they wouldn't have been able to board. The item inside the package was likely calculated to be the perfect weight. Simply put, it was for balancing the load."

After travelling halfway along the bridge, Lei reminded the passenger system to turn towards Nanshan.

"Why are we turning here?"

"This is the route recorded by the system. The... suspicious head video follows the same path. They match."

"So, in the video, another bionic gives the command to turn?"

"Uh, no. There's no voice — not human speech or machine speech."

"The criminal didn't want to leave any additional clues that could help the investigation, right? He was especially cautious about that. So, in the actual crashed vehicle, the audio of the steering command wasn't recorded. But that doesn't affect his plan — he just wanted people to think it was a malfunction of the taxi's flight control system. In his own vehicle, all he did was switch on the bionic head camera, while the route had already been pre-set."

"So, if that's the case, his alibi wouldn't hold up, would it? If it was a real-time video, he would have had to be on the same path as the crashed vehicle, even the same altitude, or else the video would have been exposed. How could he have been invisible in the surveillance footage along with the other car?"

She Loke gestured around at their surroundings.

"What are we doing right now?"

Lei Yijun paused, stunned for a moment. "You mean... was the video shot in the metaverse? This... isn't about altering the video's content. It's like creating a simulated stage for the camera. It's an audacious idea, but theoretically, it's not impossible!"

"Maybe something like that," Loke said, pulling up a quick-jump interface to famous landmarks. "Six years ago, the metaverse's civilian development only reached the second and third layers. The fourth layer just became available last year. You know the difference, right?"

"I do."

The second layer is augmented reality, and the third layer is projection, which, in layman's terms, is 3D and 4D — until the 5D layer, which includes all five senses and fully recreates the real world.

This answer wasn't as stunning as he'd hoped. It was unexpected, but still logical.

"So you're saying, the criminal played a VR projection for the bionic's head?" Lei asked.

Loke shook his head.

"Remember, that was a bionic — a digital camera. Its construction is different from human eyes. When we use one camera to film another electronic screen, the frequency difference between the digital signals causes flickering. This kind of forgery wouldn't even require high-tech forensic analysis. The human eye could spot the issue immediately. So, the criminal's method of creating an alibi in the third layer is flawed. Even today, the same trick wouldn't work with a bionic's eyes in the simulated layer."

"Then..." Lei was more confused than ever. "In the second layer... but the augmented layer is just an extension of reality, so it still doesn't solve the synchronisation issue we mentioned earlier! Could the criminal have built an identical scale filming set in the real world in such a short time?"

At this, Loke started nodding.

"The city, this stage, had already been built long ago! All they needed was to add a few weather effects and a natural projection of the scenery."

Lei Yijun was about to ask what that meant when a notification flashed on the interactive screen: *15 minutes remaining in your tour. Please finish your visit or extend for another hour.*

"Finally, let's take a night tour of the city!"

She Loke didn't answer Lei Yijun's question, instead leading them onto a luxury cruise ship.

The detective kept the suspense, making Lei feel as if his mind was buzzing with restless thoughts, like ants crawling under his skin.

Loke leaned against the side of the ship, still checking the time.

"Let's fast-forward a bit... Uncle Lei, you don't get seasick, do you?"

"I don't. And call me 'Brother', not 'Uncle'! Stop making me feel old!"

At four times the normal speed, the landscape along the two rivers quickly transformed from dots of light into a sea of brightness in the blink of an eye. Even in the heavy rain, there was a hazy beauty.

"Normally, the cruise ship would stop because of this weather, but since we're in the simulated layer, we can ignore these conditions. Let's take a look at the scene of the incident involving the vehicles..."

She Loke pointed to the Dongshuimen Yangtze River Bridge. "What time did the vehicle pass here?"

"Around 7 o'clock."

"The lights along the shore and the light show didn't start until about 7:15, and the light show on the bridge itself didn't begin until around 7:30. The vehicle passed along the side of the bridge at around 7, and given the heavy rain, the visibility at night was very low. The flight altitude would have meant that the front-facing cameras inside the car couldn't capture the view of the two shores; they would have only been able to film the main bridge pillars on the side and some blurry scenery ahead. In such heavy rain, the taxi's front windshield shouldn't have needed the wipers on. So the final visual effect would have been that the front view was almost zero, with only distant, blurry mountains visible."

Right! In an autonomous vehicle, unless they needed to see the outside scenery, the windshield wipers wouldn't have been turned on! Lei recalled the blurry images from the video.

"The large objects on the side would have captured a vague image — that's why they had to turn at almost the midpoint of the Dongshuimen Bridge, heading for their destination. Any further and the second main bridge pillar would have shown up!"

The Same Pillar

At this, She Loke gave a knowing smile, and Lei Yijun quickly realised something — there was another place in the world with the same view!

Just as they silently exchanged understanding, the cruise ship, in fast-forward, reached the Jialing River side. The Jialing River is a tributary of the Yangtze and is where the famous Hongyadong is located, on the Yuzhong Peninsula. There, there is another bridge — the Qiansimen Bridge, which only has one main bridge pillar.

And the main bridge pillar of the Qiansimen Bridge was identical to that of the Dongshuimen Bridge!

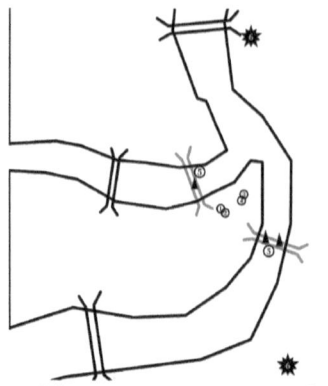
The Two Yangtze River Bridges

"The same set was built decades ago! Using the harsh weather and the darkness before the bridge's lights came on, the criminal created this 'faked reality' video. Then, he shifted to the same angle, and after reaching the same distance, he turned off the video recording. Finally, he just had to physically alter the humanoid's head and return it to the crime scene later, naturally."

No wonder there was that strange scene in the movie...

Lei had originally thought that the filmmakers included both the Qiansimen Bridge and Hongyadong in that scene because of the visual effect and the fame of the landmarks. But now, after hearing Loke's logic, he thought there was more to it — perhaps there was some deeper truth hidden inside.

Noticing that Lei Yijun had fallen into deep thought, She Loke reminded him, "We're out of time. Let's go out and talk more. You promised to take me to the station, but how about a meal first? No need to rush."

Lei Yijun was just about to say that a meal wouldn't take that long when they exited the 5D tour interface, and everything went black.

After removing the head sensor, Lei Yijun took a few seconds to adjust to the brightness of the real world. Rubbing his eyes, he asked She Loke, who was sitting beside him, "What do you want to eat? Hotpot? Can you handle spicy food—"

Turning his head, he saw Loke lying quietly, but beside him, there was suddenly an unfamiliar figure standing, seemingly unnoticed.

The man was wearing a cap, and although Lei couldn't immediately place him, he had a vague sense that he should know this person.

"How about I treat both of you to hotpot?" the man whispered, his voice steady yet tinged with a hint of mockery—while a small, gun-like object was aimed at Loke.

She Loke, however, showed no fear. He merely rolled his eyes and winked at Lei Yijun. "I felt nothing just now. He's been here for a while."

Lei instinctively reached for his waist—nothing.

My gun! But wait, he had been suspended, and all weapons were locked in the police station!

The man noticed Lei's confusion and chuckled. "It was printed. Its power isn't bad. Enough to blow this young man's head off."

"What do you want? Should I know who you are?" Lei raised his hands in surrender, not wanting to provoke the man. He asked this casually to distract him.

"Heh, I'll give your reasoning a 5 out of 10. Next, I'll give you the rest of the script."

Wait—he could hear the script? So, this man was really...

It was Wang Yuming!

"Now, this is the exciting part of the script. The man wearing the cap kills the young guy, and later, the police find that the person lying next to him, Officer Lei, was also killed by the same man. But they never suspected that the man in the cap wasn't human, but a humanoid. The humanoids's body is found in another room, with all its information wiped clean. In the end, the police discover he has the exact same face as Officer Lei." The man in the cap explained with a smirk, lifting his cap slightly.

Lei Yijun stared in shock—it looked just like his own face.

How could this be?!

"I definitely know you, because I am you."

"You—"

The imposter in front of him must have something to do with Wang Yuming—or perhaps with someone from the Oort Group. Either way, it confirmed that She Loke's reasoning was correct—the criminal was getting desperate.

How despicable! This was a human problem, yet they were using humanoids to create a crime.

But no, now wasn't the time to get angry.

Lei Yijun couldn't afford to think about when or why his identity was stolen. His only thought now was to save She Loke, who had innocently got caught up in this.

He decided to start making things up, hoping to divert the man's attention.

"If I were you, I wouldn't have waited for us to wake up and have this much of a conversation. First, I'd get rid of 'myself' and replace me with this humanoid. With the distance between us right now, I'd have a chance to subdue it. The only thing it can do now is shoot me first."

The man smiled. "Oh, not a bad idea."

Just then, a voice came from behind him, sending a chill down Lei Yijun's spine.

"How do you know I haven't already tried that? Are you so sure you're human?"

"What?"

The following words made Lei's blood run cold.

"Are all your memories of your family real? The deaths of your loved ones—are those real memories? Why can't your grandmother remember you anymore?"

Beads of sweat rolled down Lei's face as these words seemed like a curse, triggering deep memories he'd long buried.

The notice of his father's death had arrived that day when the provincial department sent someone to inform the family.

His father had been an orphan as well, which is why Lei Yijun had been raised by his grandmother. That day, his grandmother had had a terrible argument with his father—Lei Yijun couldn't remember why. His grandmother had despised his father for a long time, reportedly because "he killed her only daughter."

But Lei Yijun had always been told his mother died of an illness. There had been many discrepancies in the memory during this time. His grandmother refused to talk about it, and as a child, he didn't dare ask further questions. Only after his father passed away did he uncover some clues from his father's notes.

Those notes opened a painful box of memories for Lei Yijun. It was a scene of brutal criminals avenging their own grievances by murdering his mother in front of young Lei Yijun.

Her red dress had not originally been red—it was white.

His father had offended someone due to his job, which indirectly led to his mother's death. Lei Yijun had eventually found out that those criminals were victims of a large cryptocurrency scam, manipulated by deep-pocketed, anonymous high-tech criminals who controlled their finances and vulnerabilities, prompting them to commit terrible crimes under remote control.

Lei Yijun had sworn to find the true masterminds, no matter the cost.

As for his grandmother, she had forgotten him as Alzheimer's set in. Not that she didn't remember him; rather, seeing Lei Yijun, who looked more and more like his father, would make her hysterical. So, he had to hire someone to care for her, and he would often wear sunglasses to appear before her.

These memories... they were painful. Lei Yijun had often avoided thinking about them, pretending to forget.

But they were real—real enough to have shaped him into who he was today.

"I'm definitely human. But even if I weren't—heh, I suppose scientists would be the ones to determine that, wouldn't they?"

Lei didn't turn his head. He suppressed his curiosity about this killer who knew his past and focused on the still-dangerous She Loke.

She Loke remained obediently still, but Lei Yijun noticed his fingers were subtly moving—he was sending a message!

The gunman also noticed this, his finger slowly curling on the trigger.

It was now or never!

Without hesitation, Lei Yijun lunged.

He crashed into She Loke, pushing him aside, and sent the man who looked just like him flying.

It felt so light?

No, wait! He wasn't a humanoid?!

He was...?

Bang!

The gunshot rang out.

The fake Lei Yijun collapsed in a pool of blood.

Lei Yijun saw, with his final gaze, that the person who had been standing behind him was the 37th model—the former version of himself.

Was this the end of the story...?

Lei thought, as his vision went dark and he sank into a cold abyss.

Chapter 5
Author's Confession

O f course, the story didn't end there.

When Lei Yijun awoke, he found himself lying on a special device in the centre of a pure white room. It seemed similar to the 5D tour setup or the "Di Renjie system" login device, but more advanced.

After some moments of scratching his head, he realised there were no gunshot wounds or blood pouring out of him.

"Am I really a humanoid?" At this point, Lei Yijun couldn't tell for sure.

A familiar female voice interrupted his thoughts: "Is there anything else uncomfortable?"

Lei Yijun looked around. The door to the room opened, and Wu Mengyi walked in, followed by Shi Qingxuan.

"What's going on...?" Lei Yijun asked, touching the unfamiliar outfit he was wearing, which was covered in sensors—definitely not his usual clothes. This one was a pressure suit.

"The data collection is complete. Thank you for your cooperation," Wu Mengyi said as she called in another assistant to help remove the sensors from Lei Yijun's body.

"Data? Ah... Where's She Loke? Is he alright? The culprit? What time is it? What's the higher-ups saying?" Lei asked, his questions tumbling out.

"Sherlock?" Wu adjusted her glasses, a puzzled look crossing her face.

"That's the relative of Captain Ge—the one who calls himself a detective," Lei Yijun replied impatiently, looking at Shi.

"You are the team leader. Don't you remember?" Shi, too, seemed confused.

"Then... where's the rest of the team?" Lei couldn't sit still any longer. He stood up, pushing past an assistant, his anxiety growing as he began pacing the room.

"Besides me handling things with your grandmother, no one else has arrived. Didn't you say the celebration banquet would be after the case was officially closed?" Shi replied, sounding surprised.

"Celebration banquet?" Lei was momentarily stunned.

"The case is solved! The culprit has been caught—it's that reporter who wrote about every little detail in the novel. Didn't you say you'd know he was the culprit after watching the movie?" Shi explained.

"Oh, so it was him, after all." Lei nodded, lost in thought.

At this moment, Wu and Shi exchanged a glance, communicating something through their eyes. Nothing escaped Lei Yijun's sharp gaze.

"What's going on?" Lei asked warily.

At first, they both kept their faces serious and silent, their four eyes reflecting in a way that made Lei feel uneasy.

Then, unexpectedly, both Wu and Shi broke into laughter. Though they tried to suppress it, their behaviour only made Lei more disturbed.

"Sorry... Captain Lei, I didn't expect you to have such a bad waking mood," Shi chuckled. "It's really unprofessional, but let me laugh for a bit."

Wu Mengyi, displaying better self-control, smiled and explained lightly, "Although memory confusion is common when entering the virtual layer for the first time, your reaction is quite interesting. I'll make sure to record it."

As she spoke, she tapped something on her tablet.

"Virtual layer?" Lei echoed, puzzled.

"Yes, this is the prototype of the Dreamoscope. The virtual layer is the fifth layer of the metaverse, which hasn't been opened to the public yet—it's a completely virtual world constructed from human memories. It's directly input into the brain to create an immersive virtual environment. After Inspector Xia arrested the suspect, you came to help me collect data with this machine," Wu explained.

"So, I wasn't shot? What about the humanoids?" Lei pressed.

"After you submitted your resignation, you never left the police building. As for the final scene—it was Officer Shi's idea. You should ask him about it."

"Ah-hum." Shi Qingxuan cleared his throat and elaborated, "We compared the new No.37 humanoids with others in a cross-reference experiment. After inputting known case details, some of them could deduce the criminal methods based on logic and common sense. In terms of intelligence, these humanoids are very advanced. However, they can't sacrifice themselves to protect the public in a battle of wits with criminals. In the end, none of them demonstrated human emotions. I've already submitted the report."

"Ah, so that kid's fine, then?" Lei relaxed, letting out a deep sigh.

"Loke is still in Shanghai. Ge had approval from the higher-ups for him to access this special virtual space as a tourist. The case details were only revealed to him after you cracked the case, but his conclusions during real-time simulation really impressed everyone. You asked me to let him join the review process, don't you remember?" Wu Mengyi continued.

"Now that I think about it, I do vaguely remember..." Lei reflected. "Also, that last part felt a bit abrupt. It had too many signs of being made up. Grandmother... Ah... so you didn't notice that, either."

"Made-up stories?" Shi shrugged. "I'm no good at that. It's the filmmakers who are good at it. Apparently, some people in the metaverse can randomly adapt and speak in ways that sound completely real."

"Yeah, some people just like to make things up," Lei muttered, putting on his jacket and patting the inside pocket. He pulled out the notebook left by his father.

The aged leather felt so real. It couldn't possibly be fake. He flipped it open casually. The pages were filled with his father's "observation journals" documenting his growth. But on the last page with writing, a childish hand had scribbled a symbol: **W.** The symbol was surrounded by circles, with such pressure that it nearly pierced through the paper.

Could this be connected to the case? Lei held onto a glimmer of hope.

"What did the suspect say?" he asked.

"He said everything. A person like him would love to show off his 'perfect methods.' This confession seals the deal. There's no question about the conviction," Wu replied.

"Let's go meet him," Lei said, determination in his eyes.

◆

This was one of the strangest suspects Lei Yijun had encountered in his career.

"What else do you want to know?" The suspect, Wang Yuming, said eagerly as soon as he saw someone had come in to question him. From his expression, it was clear that he was excited and eager to talk.

Wang Yuming was a human male, under thirty, with no mechanical modifications. His appearance was unremarkable; his hairstyle was slightly trendy, though a bit messy from neglect. His clothing was simple and casual, his sneakers quite expensive, and he wore a pair of clear lens glasses. According to the database, he was a freelance creator, novelist, journalist, and the writer and the planner for several live-streaming shows. He had no criminal record whatsoever, from birth to the present.

"What's your purpose?" Lei asked.

For people like him, it was better to let them talk freely, Lei thought to himself. Perhaps something unexpected would come up.

Seeing that it was Lei who entered, Wang's lips curled slightly in a smile.

"You've finally arrived. I've been observing you for a long time," he said.

That response sent a chill down Lei's spine, and an inner feeling of disgust slowly spread. However, he kept his professional composure and didn't let it show.

"Are you working for Oort?" Lei pressed.

"Strictly speaking, not just them. I work for many people, earning my keep. But that's just business transactions. True creativity can't be tainted by such mundane things," Wang replied, his tone almost disdainful.

Lei Yijun didn't want to continue down that path, so he remained silent and let Wang Yuming speak for himself.

As expected, Wang Yuming didn't disappoint.

"From the results, Oort stands to gain the most from this incident. However, if you dig deeper, you'll find that the core team of Momo Controls suffered huge losses, betrayed their boss, and later joined Oort Group."

"Didn't the shareholders of Momo Controls sue them?" Lei asked, raising an eyebrow.

"Actually, the major shareholders of Momo Controls already exited early through initial financing and stock market profits. They offloaded their negative assets before the real losses occurred. It's classic shell game tactics—an escape just in time," Wang explained.

Lei frowned, his thoughts racing. "So..."

"The core asset of a high-tech enterprise is its people—more precisely, the creativity of its people. A tech company without people is just an empty shell. But when the core team doesn't receive corresponding returns for the value they create, they are forced to take desperate measures. Do you think that's fair?" Wang continued, his eyes gleaming with a strange sort of conviction.

Lei had never considered the issue from this angle before. For a moment, he was at a loss for words.

Wang Yuming didn't let up.

"The taxi company was ordered to reform, but the system that replaced the old one—well, it's the same technology from the same people. How many secrets are hidden behind that? I don't know either. Oh, by the way, after the environmental monitoring bureau criticised the cheap semi-solid batteries used in older models, the entire industry has been under pressure to shift towards all-solid-state batteries. The product iterations and the resulting job creation, and GDP growth—who do you think profits from that? As for that unlucky fool who was fired— the hush money he got is probably something he'll never be able to earn in his entire life!"

"Finally, this movie has sparked a major societal debate about the potential problems robots could cause. In the near future, we'll inevitably face this question: Do they have the same personality and rights as us? Sure, even the most advanced humanoids today are still just heaps of scrap metal, but how can we ignore it, not prepare for it?" Wang finished, his tone almost philosophical.

Lei Yijun kept his focus on the various tags displayed on the system's interface—the ones the interrogated person couldn't see. The different coloured labels and values represented various indicators that the investigative team was monitoring.

The orange polygraph indicators were normal, meaning Wang wasn't intentionally concealing anything that he should have known.

What he said was credible, logical.

But still...

"Since you've confessed to your actions, we will hand you over to the prosecution. We won't discuss these sociological issues with you. One final question: Why did you choose those two humanoids?" Lei asked.

Wang Yuming smiled.

"Ah, you want to ask about your personal connection to this? Oh, no, it was truly just a coincidence. The two models of service humanoids happened to be perfect for my plan. After applying for disposal funds from Oort, I acted independently. I only needed two defective products to pull off a scheme worth billions! But during my visit to the nursing home, under the guise of an interview, I learned about your situation. I had a 'chat' with it, and that's that. This part of the script I wrote myself," Wang said nonchalantly.

The humanoids knew why Lei Yijun couldn't accompany his grandmother and had been trained to use this detail in their language processing—something Lei Yijun never imagined would be exploited by a criminal.

If Unit No.37 had not been used for corporate espionage but instead to target him... how many innocent people could have been affected?

Lei turned to leave, no longer willing to engage with this psychopath who believed he could control others through his script.

"W."

The word Wang Yuming uttered made Lei Yijun stop dead in his tracks.

He slowly turned back, looking at Wang, whose face still bore that eerie smile.

"What does that mean?" Lei asked, his voice tight.

"I just said that part of the script was my creation. But the original outline for the whole script—W wrote it a long time ago," Wang said.

"W... What is W?" Lei demanded.

"I don't know. Maybe it's short for 'Writer'? I just followed the outline W set. You'll find the answer at the deepest point of the metaverse." Wang waved dismissively, as if it were no big deal.

Lei Yijun was desperate to know what "W" was, but the suspect refused to speak further. The entire Special Tech-Crimes Action Team couldn't get him to talk, and even the "Di Renjie System" failed in front of a brain locked in absolute secrecy.

After that, Wang Yuming didn't say another word. It was as if he had been muted by the system itself—forever silent, leaving only an empty shell, mysteriously smiling at humanity.

Clearly, the author had once again planted a seed for a future plot twist, one that author had no intention of resolving right now.

Epilogue

After everything had ended, Lei Yijun returned to the Yishan Nursing Home. He had instructed the staff to replace the humanoid that had been caring for his grandmother with a standard caregiver model—he decided to visit her more often from now on.

His grandmother was unaffected by the events that had unfolded. At that moment, she sat by the window, shelling sunflower seeds, occasionally glancing at the large screen where a decades-old TV drama was playing.

She noticed him as soon as he walked in.

"Lei, you're back," she said.

Lei Yijun froze.

"Why are you wearing sunglasses indoors... oh, you're getting married tomorrow, aren't you? Let your future mother-in-law say a few words..."

The police officer walked over, his voice trembling slightly as he responded, "Mom, I'm listening. Please go ahead."

◆

The mystery of "W" was something Lei Yijun knew he couldn't solve in the short term. But he had no time to dwell on it. His superior had instructed him to submit a detailed case review report on the Nanshan 716 autonomous taxi crash—of course, because of confidentiality, it had to be entirely his own work, with no AI assistance.

Lei Yijun, who was notoriously bad at writing official documents, sat in his dorm, pulling at his hair in frustration, trying to get the information from his mind into the computer.

"I wish I were a robot right now!" he sighed.

Meanwhile, the network news broadcast the final announcement: Wang Yuming, male, 39 years old, was suspected of using his position as a journalist to damage private property in order to acquire insider trading information, with significant negative impact. The police had arrested the suspect, and further investigations would be shared via official announcements.

Other related companies and individuals had not yet been sued. Lei knew that such legal proceedings would only begin after his entire team completed their reports.

He wasn't sure when they'd all get together for the hotpot again...

But as soon as he thought about how his investigation might indirectly affect thousands of people, the pressure on Lei Yijun skyrocketed. He wasn't like Wang Yuming—he didn't have the confidence of a scriptwriter who could control everything.

So, the police officer decided to take a break and play a game to relieve his stress. He logged into the Metaverse using a Dreamoscope Dr Wu had given him (Wu Mengyi still needed to collect his data). However, Lei clearly didn't want to turn on the data synchronisation switch just yet—he simply wanted to play an FPS game and clear his head!

Too lazy to design a new virtual avatar, he opted for the one he had used when sampling his personal profile for Model No.37—perfectly reasonable, since when playing such games, it's best to use an avatar that reflects your own body type!

Next, Lei Yijun randomly selected a sci-fi city-themed shooting game.

He thought to himself: *I scored full marks in shooting at the police academy. Dealing with amateurs should be like chopping vegetables, right?*

But to his surprise, within minutes, he was shot in the head and instantly killed.

"Are you kidding me? Who's hacking? I'm reporting you!" Lei shouted, as his virtual body lay motionless on the ground.

Just as he was about to log out of the server to report his opponent, he noticed a familiar figure approaching his virtual corpse.

The silver-white hair, the agile figure, and that unrealistically handsome face.

For some reason, despite having never met in the real world, it felt as though they had already become good friends...

"Lei, bro, you're so weak! I saw you poke your head out, and I thought we were about to have an epic battle!" came the familiar teasing voice.

Another BAD friend!

Trying to save his own image, Lei could only awkwardly respond, "I have a case I want your help with... Well, it's personal. So, I had to come find you quietly."

"Why didn't you tell me earlier?"

The detective's eyes sparkled with excitement.

At that time, Lei Yijun had no idea that this person wasn't just a detective in the virtual world; She Loke was also a super player.

Also, the police officer had no inkling that the story of the Metaverse Detective was only just beginning, and it would stretch on for a very long time.

Afterword

On some of the scientific elements in this work and my creative journey:

To bridge the gap between real-world technological advancements and the speculative frontiers of a fictional future, I naturally drew upon some technologies I encountered during my educational background.

I hold a bachelor's degree in Electrical Engineering, with a graduation project related to indoor service delivery robots. Later, I pursued a master's degree in Multimedia Information Technology, where I also explored fields like computer vision and emotion analysis using brain-computer interfaces in gaming. After graduation, I worked for a major big-tech company and have since produced and released several games.

Initially, when writing the main series, my focus was purely from a gaming industry perspective, aiming to depict my vision of the entangled future of technology, entertainment, and humanity in the metaverse. However, when creating this prequel, which connects reality with a fictional future, I found myself linking all the knowledge I had learned in the past.

As you will notice after reading the story, I have a very positive view of robots and androids—at least I don't see them as monsters to be feared. After all, I've built adorable little robots myself! That said, I am also deeply concerned and can foresee them being misused for criminal soon.

Regarding computer vision and brain-computer interfaces, these topics are touched upon lightly in this prequel. However, the layered prototype of the metaverse introduced here will evolve into the central stage in the forthcoming main series episodes, no longer serving as just a backdrop.

Ten years ago, during my university days, I encountered electric vehicles and service robots, which are now (in 2024) integrated into many aspects of human society. AI and cryptos, needless to say, are today's hottest technological topics. I intend to incorporate my thoughts on these technologies into future works.

Of course, I am by no means an expert in all scientific fields. Many of the settings and plotlines are crafted to serve the story and character development. This is the charm of science fiction: bold hypotheses, thoughtful realisation.

If there are any inaccuracies in my understanding, I hope experts can use this popular entertainment work as an opportunity to show the public about these technologies. I would be delighted if this story could serve as a springboard for greater awareness. Popular entertainment should not stand in opposition to scientific theory—it is one of the best mediums for its dissemination.

If, after reading this, you find yourself looking forward to future works, please follow me on social media and share your thoughts with others!

Many thanks!
W.J.

About the author

W.J. SAM

W. J. Sam (They) has a keen interest in science and societal themes, embodying a novelist deeply engrossed in the realms of science fiction and fantasy, with a pronounced affection for anime.

If you are interested, please subscribe to WJ's mailing list to stay updated on her latest works. https://subscribepage.io/wjsamjoin

Visit their official website for more information: https://helioswriter.com/

Also, you may follow WJ on SNS:

f facebook.com/profile.php?id=100095301944901

O instagram.com/authorwjsam

Acknowledgements

Special thanks to my former colleague and lifestyle mentor, Ran, as well as my local friend, Miao, for showing me around this magical city I last visited when I was five years old.

Heartfelt gratitude also goes to the Taoist masters of Laojundong Temple in Nanshan, Chongqing, and the blessings of the celestial gods, through whom I received an auspicious fortune ticket for this work. While this is a work focused on technology and materialism, I hold great respect for the local customs and beliefs. I also hope to integrate these traditional cultures into the vision of future technology.

This is a work of fiction.

Names, characters, places, and incidents either are products of the author's imagination or are used fictitiously. Any similarity to actual events or locales or persons, living or dead, is entirely coincidental.

Neo Chongqing Glitch

Copyright © 2024 by W.J. Sam

All rights reserved.

No part of this publication may be reproduced, distributed, or transmitted in any form or by any means, including photocopying, recording, or other electronic or mechanical methods, without the prior written permission of the publisher, except in the case of brief quotations embodied in critical reviews and certain other noncommercial uses permitted by copyright law.

Published by

HELIOPOLIS PRESS

Unit B, 12F, 28 Yee Wo Street, Causeway Bay, Hong Kong

www.heliopolis.press

Heliopolis Press® is a registered trademark of

Heliopolis Creative and Culture Limited

www.heliopolis-cc.com

The Hong Kong Public Library has cataloged the **paperback** edition as follows:

Name: Sam, W.J.. Author.

Title: Neo Chongqing Glitch / W.J. Sam.

Description: First edition. | Hong Kong: Heliopolis Press, 2024.

Identifiers: ISBN 978-988-70531-4-9 (eBook)

Identifiers: ISBN 978-988-70531-6-3 (Hardcover)

Subjects: Science Fiction | Mystery

Classification: F | Fiction

ISBN 978-988-70531-3-2 (Paperback)

First Edition: November, 2024

First Hardcover Edition: November, 2024

Printed in Hong Kong

Our books may be purchased in bulk for promotional, educational, or business use. Please contact your local bookseller or the Heliopolis Press Sales Department by email at sale@heliopolis.press

www.ingramcontent.com/pod-product-compliance
Lightning Source LLC
LaVergne TN
LVHW041533070526
838199LV00046B/1652